This book

The Paleface Killer

Brett Conroy, the gun-slinging boss of the town of Macey's Folly, finds his iron grip on the settlement slipping away when a mysterious stranger arrives. His chief gunman makes the mistake of thinking the stranger is only a city dude and soon comes to regret his error.

Aided by the shyster lawyer Elias Marlin plus a crooked mayor and sheriff, Conroy tries every brutal trick to get rid of the stranger. But the stranger swears to destroy Conroy's hold on the town and names himself 'The Paleface Killer'.

When the courageous Tracey Lee throws in her lot with the puzzling stranger, the scene becomes set for a maelstrom of murder and mayhem, which few will survive.

The Paleface Killer

PHILIP HARBOTTLE

A Black Horse Western

ROBERT HALE · LONDON

© Philip Harbottle 2004
First published in Great Britain 2004

ISBN 0 7090 7419 0

Robert Hale Limited
Clerkenwell House
Clerkenwell Green
London EC1R 0HT

Typeset by
Derek Doyle & Associates, Liverpool.
Printed and bound in Great Britain by
Antony Rowe Limited, Wiltshire

To my uncles – Bill, Fred, John, Robert and Tom Hardwick and Sid Robertson

1

STRANGER IN TOWN

Macey's Folly lay at the foot of a large mountain range, an unplanned huddle of mainly wooden buildings, with the most notable being the Swaying Hip saloon and a large general stores. The small town had mushroomed up after one Clem Macey had started a spurious gold rush. Spreads had been established on the rich pastureland just outside the town. Now its expansion was halted, and the ramshackle town lay rotting in the intense Arizona sunshine in summer, slowly deteriorating in the midst of heavy winter rains.

If few people now remembered the town, even fewer knew that it was run on gun law by Brett Conroy, current owner of the Swaying Hip. The previous owner had lost all interest after he had been shot through the heart by Conroy, whose rule over the township was absolute.

A couple of wooden shanties and a portable pair of damaged steps did duty as a railway station. Visitors were few and far between, but somehow the news had gotten around that a visitor was expected.

The man detailed to watch for him was a sun-wizened

old-timer who 'managed' the railroad halt – hardly a demanding job, since barely two trains a month ever stopped there. But whoever the stranger was, he needed to be put in his place.

The lone man who alighted in the early summer evening was young, loose jointed, with heavy shoulders and large hands. He was dressed incongruously in a conventional Western shirt and very clean tweed trousers. The spotless trousers smacked more of the city than the open spaces. Beneath his obviously new Stetson lay thick blond hair. If not exactly handsome, his powerful jaw and apparent rugged strength at least marked him as interesting. He was carrying a suitcase, and at his waist hung twin pearl-handled .45s in crossover belts.

As the sounds of the departing train faded the young man glanced about him, his expression indicating he was not impressed with his survey. He moved forward slowly and halted at the first wooden shanty, where the old-timer waited in his dusty uniform-cap, his eyes narrowed suspiciously. The only people in Macey's Folly who kept their personal history to themselves were those who knew how to handle their guns and to silence anyone asking too many questions – such as Brett Conroy.

'Travelled far, mister?' the old-timer asked, taking the small roll of paper which served as a ticket.

'It's on the ticket,' the young man said briefly, motioning to it. His voice was surly, but passably well educated. 'Or can't you read?'

'OK, mister, no need to git tough about it, is there?' The oldster realized that it was going to be no easy task to dig information out of this awkward new arrival.

'Taking you long enough to fix that ticket, isn't it?' the man demanded. 'I thought this was journey's end . . . this dump is Macey's Folly, isn't it?'

'Sure it is,' the ancient agreed, staring at the ticket

whilst he struggled to get his thoughts in focus. 'An' lookee-here, young feller, I only asked a civil question, see? Mmmm, from Jefferson City, eh? Quite a ways off. Seems t'me you ain't no outdoors man, neither.'

'What the hell business is it of yours? Anyhow, how come that you can tell?'

'Listen, son, outdoorsmen git this blasted sun burned inter their skins – but you're still kinda pasty. City guy, I'd say.'

'I may be "pasty", but I shot two men in Jefferson City, before I headed in this direction,' the young man said deliberately. 'I didn't like the way they did business. That satisfy you?'

The ancient blinked, nearly dropping the ticket roll.

'Tough guy, huh? Well, that ain't exactly novel round here – not with Brett Conroy runnin' the town. He's about the fastest draw there is . . . .'

'Not necessarily. *I*'m here now.' Then, before the old man could ask any more questions, the young man added harshly: 'Where in this hole does a man find a place in which to stay?'

'Reckon you could try Ma Barrett. Her roomin'-house is in the main street, straight across from the Swayin' Hip. Guess she ain't too fussy about the kind of boarders she has.'

'Thanks. But I'm not sure I cared for the way you said that.'

'No offence, son,' the old man said hastily. 'But you did say yourself you was a killer on the run, after all.'

The young stranger did not reply. Instead he turned and strode away, leaving the old man trying to puzzle out in his cobwebby mentality whether he was really danger- ous or just slinging a line. He certainly seemed self-assured enough. . . .

Moving away from the station, the young man followed

a cinder track towards the town, occasionally stopping to assess his surroundings. At the top of the rise the town lay before him, the mountains to its rear. As he neared the town, the evening sun gradually dipped, until at last he was in shadow and the unprepossessing main street became cloaked in gathering purple mist, with a mixture of shadows and dappled patches of sunlight.

There was more activity than he'd suspected from a distance. Macey's Folly was far from derelict. Several men were lounging around, just trying to cool their sun-fried brains now the evening had come. There were a number of men and women in the main street itself, and the boardwalks carried their complement of inhabitants – chiefly men – lounging on the boardwalk rail, talking or smoking, and seeming to be looking at nothing in particular, until they raised their eyes and nudged each other as a particularly lissom girl of the West happened to pass by.

Because the young man was a stranger in town – and pale-faced at that – he attracted a certain amount of attention. Women glanced and kept on walking, but the men stared and elbowed each other, some of them grinning. As he was passing a bunch of cowpokes sprawling against the boardwalk rail, the young man caught one of the men in the act of making faces. He stopped, then returned to where the group was standing.

'Enjoying yourself, feller?' he asked quietly.

The cowpoke he addressed did not answer. He was tough-looking, unshaven, with broad shoulders and hair the colour of a newly dug carrot.

'I asked a question,' the young man added. 'Didn't you understand me? Or are you too young to talk?'

One of the men guffawed – only to smother it as the young man glared at him.

'A guy can make faces if he likes,' the red-haired man

responded lazily.

'Listen, cowboy – I don't happen to like it.'

The cowpoke grinned all the more broadly, winking at his lounging comrades.

'Guess yuh don't know who you're talkin' to, feller. I'm Smoke Milligan, Brett Conroy's right-hand man.'

'So what?' the young man enquired.

'So this— You'd better blow! I've no time for city dudes with their fancy pants. An' if you live long enough around here you'll find that a pantywaist in Macey's Folly is liable to be chucked in the horse trough.'

The young man considered, his suitcase still in his left hand. Abruptly his right slammed up in a bunched fist and took Smoke Milligan clean on the jaw. It was a punch of power and precision. Smoke gave a roar of pain and, unable to save himself, toppled backwards over the low rail and crashed into the dusty street.

As his colleagues gaped in amazement, one of them twisted back sharply, ready for murder – only to find that the young stranger had already drawn his right-hand gun and was holding it steadily.

'You hoodlums had better watch your manners. Any more insolence from you and I'll blast the dirt from under you. Savvy?'

The men just stared, astonished. Smoke still lay dazedly where he had fallen, his eyes narrowed and his jaw feeling about to drop off at any moment.

'If I ever see you again, better see that you behave like gentlemen.' With that the young man releathered his gun, gripped his suitcase, and went on his way along the board-walk, before vanishing into the doorway of Ma Barrett's rooming-house.

Smoke Milligan scrambled up painfully from the dust and breathed hard, then he tossed back his tumbled red hair and glared at his companions.

11

'Who in blue hell does that guy think he is?' he demanded, scowling as he slowly regained the boardwalk.

'Dunno,' one of the men answered. 'Seems to me that old Seth at the railroad halt has slipped up in not warning us about him.'

'Mighty handy with his fist, too,' another remarked drily. 'You sure swallowed that one, Smoke.'

'Shut your mouth!' Smoke spat. 'That punch was a fluke. I just wasn't ready for it.'

'Seems to me,' yet another commented, 'that you had plenty of time. Standin' right next to the guy, you oughta seen what was comin'!'

'Shut up,' Smoke said sourly. 'The next time that guy tries anythin' I'll kill him. But first I reckon the boss oughta know about this. Let's go.'

The man smiled cynically. He was thinking that the boss wasn't going to be so sweet on his best gunman when he heard what had happened.

Smoke led the way across the main street and finally through the batwings of the Swaying Hip. The place was almost empty, and the barkeeps were polishing glasses whilst Brett Conroy himself, the owner, was in his favourite position by one of the ornamental pillars.

In the midst of selecting one of his long Mexican cheroots, he glanced up briefly, then he deliberately finished lighting his cheroot. He was a big, swarthy man, with piercing dark eyes, hooked nose, and wavy black hair. The almost-handsome effect was spoiled by a vicious, rat-trap mouth.

'What do you lot want?' he asked shortly, as the men gathered around him. 'Spit it out and then blow. You're making the place untidy.'

'Something you oughta know,' Smoke said acidly. 'There's a guy blown into town who looks set on making trouble. Old Seth was supposed to tell us when any

12

stranger showed, but this guy musta been too quick for him. He's dangerous, boss!'

'Yeah? Like the others he'll soon find out that I'm the boss around here and—'

'This guy's different,' Smoke said stubbornly. Then, as he hesitated, one of the men said it for him:

'The guy nearly cracked Smoke's jaw for just grinnin' at him. Whammed him right over the boardwalk rail. I never saw a punch like it.'

Conroy's eyes narrowed. 'First time I've heard of you being caught out, Smoke. Sort of destroys my faith in you.'

'He acted so fast I didn't have time to see it comin'—'

'What's this mug's name?'

'He didn't say. Got a suitcase and usual hardware. Finished up in Ma Barrett's, so I guess he's aimin' to stay.'

'Mmmm . . .' Conroy fingered his square chin. 'He may be just passing through after staying the night, or mebbe he's this guy we've heard of who figured on coming here. He may be something we can't tolerate. A marshal, for instance.'

A law officer in Macey's Folly was the last thing the gang wanted. With Conroy mixed up in all manner of dubious deals, if the law fingered him, it would inevitably get them as well. Cattle, traffic in gold, even stage hold-ups and railroad robberies – though apparently not even remotely connected with him – could in the final analysis be laid at his door. The very mention of the word marshal was cause for concern.

'I could take him out,' Smoke said, drawing his .45 and considering it.

'Put that rod back, you bonehead!' Conroy motioned impatiently. 'If we rub out a lawman we'll have the authorities breathing down our necks. The best course is to sound out this critter first.'

'Over at Ma Barrett's?'

'No, we'll wait until he comes in here – unless he's one of these lilywhites who don't drink. And if he doesn't come in here and moves out after dossing for the night we'll let it go at that.'

'But I owe that guy plenty!' Smoke objected. 'I ain't takin' a back dive like I did and lettin' the critter just walk out of town.'

'You'll do as I say,' Conroy said ominously. 'But if the guy does hang around, then you can hit back. Wish I'd seen you fall over that rail. Knock some of the darned swagger out of you, mebbe.'

Smoke muttered something and turned away to the bar.

Meantime, the young man who had caused all the consternation was in the hallway of Ma Barrett's, talking to that fat, but clean-looking elderly woman herself.

'From the look of this advance rent money, son, you must be figuring on staying some time,' she said, folding the greenbacks and putting them in her apron pocket.

'Yes,' the young man agreed. 'I have important business in this district.'

'All right with me. Most of my guests disappear before I can collect. You sound like an eddicated feller. From the city mebbe?'

'Jefferson City. The name's' – the young man hesitated – 'Dirk Manning. It's not my real name, but it's good enough for these parts. I've powerful reasons for wanting to keep my real name quiet.'

'What did you do? Murder a guy?' Ma Barrett's tact was not her strong point.

'*Yes!*' The young man's mouth set harshly. 'I killed two men who tried to double-cross me. I believe in killing things that annoy me. Only logical, isn't it? Doctors kill diseases, I guess, and some men are like diseases.'

'Sure, sure.' Ma Barrett was struggling not to look bewildered. After an awkward pause, she said: 'Disease

14

and men ain't the same thing.'

'I know. Anyone who kills a disease is a hero. But if you kill a man who ain't fit to live you're an outlaw – or else star guest at a necktie party.'

'I – er – I'll show you your room,' Ma Barrett said uneasily, and turned to the stairs.

Manning looked around the room, and found it surprisingly clean. He nodded in satisfaction, then put his suitcase down and turned to the woman.

'I noticed that you pulled a face back there when I mentioned having killed two men. What's the problem? Murder and bullets ain't exactly new around this town, are they?'

'Guess not, son. Macey's Folly has been built on hot lead and gin – but it still gave me a shock to find you a killer too.'

'Listen, Ma. Every man's a killer deep down. Only some just think about it, whilst others do it.' Dirk Manning smiled grimly. 'Why didn't you think I was a killer?'

'You just don't look the part. City manners, not many slugs in your gun belts, good clothes and suitcase. Not like most of these unshaven buzzards in Macey's Folly here.' Ma Barrett sighed and moved to the doorway. 'When I first saw you I thought I'd gotten me a different sort of guest at last. It hurts to find I'm wrong.'

Manning shrugged, his expression uncompromising. Then: 'Where can I get more slugs for my gun belts? A guy needs ammunition in this town. On my way here I had to take care of a grinning hoodlum called Smoke Milligan – and only had my fists to do it with.'

'But he's Brett Conroy's right-hand man!' Ma gasped. 'Conroy runs this town, and I've known him shoot a man down for a darned sight less. Even if you have got business in Macey's Folly, I'd advise you to get out pronto!'

'I'm not afraid of Conroy. I'm staying here while I

complete my business. I'd have been here even sooner but for being in jail. Now, where can I get slugs?'

'Jud Halloran's place.' Ma spoke reluctantly. 'Three doors away. If he's closed, you can knock on the house door. I guess he won't turn business away.'

Manning nodded. 'Thanks. So Conroy runs the town, huh? I already heard as much from that ancient ruin at the railroad halt. He said Conroy gets away with it because he's supposed to be faster on the draw than any man in town.'

'He *is*.' Ma's voice was sombre. 'My old man thought he could outdraw him before today and guessed wrong. He's still alive – just – and he won't ever forget.' The woman paused, then added seriously: 'Don't try conclusions with Conroy, son – he'll fill you full of lead before you know it. I wouldn't like that.'

'Thanks,' Manning said drily. 'The business I'm on in this town may result in plenty of gun play – but I'm not exactly unversed in the art myself. Conroy doesn't worry me.'

'All right, I've said my piece. Anythin' more you want to know about this town before I leave you to it?'

'Where can I get a horse?'

'There's a livery stable end of the street. Open all hours. You can hire a horse and stable it in the yard if you want.'

'Thanks, Ma. One more thing. When do we eat?'

'Give me fifteen minutes.'

'Good! Gives me time to see about those slugs and a horse.'

Manning followed Ma Barrett down the stairs and then went out to the boardwalk and along to the livery stable. He came back with a horse, stabled it in the yard, and then continued on his way to the gunsmith's.

Darkness had fallen and the kerosene lamps were flaring smokily from the timber uprights lining the main street. But Manning knew he was being watched. Men, apparently just lounging, were dotted in various parts of the street. Evidently Brett Conroy's army of gunhawks and snoopers had orders to keep a bead on the tough, mysterious stranger.

Jud Halloran did not at all like the idea of opening after hours but the sight of a roll of greenbacks soon changed his mind. Since Halloran was also the local undertaker, any business with guns was usually to his later further advantage.

He led the way into his stores and set the oil-lamp burning. Then he brought forth a selection of his wares and waited while Manning carefully selected the make of slugs he wanted. Ten minutes later, his purchase completed, Manning emerged again. Except for his city-type trousers he looked normal for the region, the .45s still swinging at his hips – but now his belts were loaded and he also carried extra supplies of bullets in the cardboard box under his arm. He still had the same assured walk.

'Pretty, ain't he?' Smoke Mulligan spat. He was leaning against the post nearest the Swaying Hip, a few of his satellites around him. From here they had a good view of Ma Barrett's and Jud Halloran's, the kerosene lights picking out Manning clearly enough.

'Wonder what the heck he wants in Macey's Folly?' one the satellites murmured. 'I've a suspicion the boss knows but he sure won't tell us.'

Smoke only grunted, then frowned with disappointment as the stranger turned off into Ma Barrett's and failed to reappear – for the simple reason that he was tackling a man-sized meal. It had been specially prepared for him.

'In future,' Ma Barrett said, as she brought in coffee, 'you'll stick to the hours, son. Supper's at sundown and breakfast's at seven.' She considered him in the lamplight,

17

the glow casting on to her enormous bosom, then added: 'Did you get those slugs?'

Manning patted his belts. 'Sure thing! From the number of hard-boiled critters watching me out there, I may have to shoot sooner than I figured. Just what are Conroy's men all so leery of?'

'Afraid of being caught by the law. Conroy is the biggest crook hereabouts. Not only in the dues he levels on homesteaders through the mayor, who fixes the taxes, but also the cattle- and horse-trading he does. Leastways he calls it trading: thieving more like.'

'Yet nobody does anything about it?'

'Depends who you are. That's what the boys are leery of Mebbe you smell like a marshal to them.'

'I'm no marshal. I'm as scared of a marshal as these mugs in Macey's Folly. Mebbe they'd feel kinder to me if they knew that. . . .' Manning ate for a while as he thought something out, then: 'Do you happen to know of the Double Triangle ranch hereabouts?'

'Double Triangle? Why, sure! About three miles down the trail. Used to be owned by Clint Dawson 'til his heart gave up an' he passed out. Why? Did you know him?'

'Mebbe . . . I just wondered. Pretty good spread he had, huh?'

'Biggest hereabouts – about five thousand head and prosperin' well, especially since Haslam took over.'

Manning stopped eating and glanced up, a queer light in his hard blue eyes. 'Haslam?'

Ma Barrett nodded. 'Yeah – Nat Haslam, and his step-daughter.'

Manning remained silent, his face expressionless. He did not ask any more questions; instead he resumed eating. Ma Barrett lumbered back to her own quarters, and presently she heard the slam of the screen door as Manning left the rooming-house, having finished his meal.

Outside he rolled himself a cigarette, looking up and down the boardwalk. The knots of men who had been watching him had vanished, possibly into the noisy interior of Brett Conroy's gin palace. Manning lighted his cigarette, then strode to the Swaying Hip. He passed through the batwings, the twin .45s slapping against his thighs as he headed towards the bar counter.

The drinkers there looked at him, then at each other, then back to him again. All they encountered was the flinty stare of his blue eyes. He stood out in the assembly, from his unseasoned complexion to the tweed pants he was still wearing.

'Remember me, feller?' Smoke Milligan came sidling up and leaned on the bar counter.

Manning took the whiskey the barkeep handed him, downed it, then considered Smoke pensively. 'With an ugly face like yours, you're kind of hard to forget.'

'Why, you damned city slicker, keep talkin' to me like that and I'll let yuh have it!'

'Have what?' Manning asked calmly. 'Whether it be your gun or your fists, my friend, you know I'm a darned sight too quick for you.'

'Yeah? That's what you think—'

As he broke off in mid-sentence, Smoke's hand blurred down to his gun but before he could grasp it and whip it up, he found himself staring directly into the barrel of Manning's own levelled .45.

'You were saying?' Manning asked softly. Smoke took his hand away from his holster. There was a look of dazed awe on his face that was almost comical.

'Your jaw's on the floor, Smoke,' Manning remarked. 'That's where the rest of you would be too if you'd tried firing that gun.'

'That's enough of your stupidity, Smoke!'

Brett Conroy appeared at that moment, coming slowly

forward from his usual stand beside the ornamental pillar. 'Get out of my way, Smoke,' he ordered briefly. 'Leave this to me.'

Smoke muttered venomously under his breath, but did as he was told. Manning calmly turned back to his drink. Then he paused with his glass half-way to his lips as Conroy spoke to him, his vicious mouth twisted into an unconvincing smile.

'I'm apologizing for Smoke, stranger. He ain't got no manners.'

'Or looks neither.'

Conroy grinned round his cheroot. 'Right. I never did reckon much to Smoke's pan myself. I keep him around because he happens to be useful when guys get a bit outa hand – if you know what I mean?' Manning did not say anything. He continued drinking his whiskey, elbow on the bar counter.

'Don't talk much, do you?' Conroy asked, with ill-concealed irritation.

'I'm just trying to figure out what you meant. You didn't really come over here just to discuss that gun-happy clown, did you?'

'Nope – something more than that. Have another drink – on the house.'

Conroy motioned his hand and another glass of whiskey was brought. Manning downed a couple more mouthfuls without blinking. Then he looked fixedly at Conroy and raised an eyebrow.

'I own this saloon,' Conroy said deliberately, his smile now gone. 'Just as I own nearly all the town as well. And what I don't own, I *rule*. Savvy?'

'Mebbe your big talk goes down OK with these hayseeds, but it doesn't register with me,' Manning said. 'No man's so big that there isn't somebody bigger.'

Conroy took a drink himself, his eyes narrowed. 'I ain't

sure whether you're trying to pick a quarrel or defending yourself by talking tough. You'd best remember that I'm absolute boss of this town, and if any man – or woman either for that matter – gets in my way I just stamp on their faces.'

'So what?'

'So I want to know what you're doing in Macey's Folly. And you'd better give me the right answer.'

Manning jerked out his tobacco-packet and rolled another of his cigarettes deliberately. He did not look at his fingers whilst he worked: instead he stared insolently at Conroy. Finally he gave a grim smile.

'What's the matter, Conroy? Frightened that if I stay too long I might find out too much?'

Conroy's face darkened. 'Ain't nothing for you to find out, stranger.'

'That isn't what I've heard.'

The studied insolence of this man was making Conroy's trigger-finger itch, but he still did not use his gun. He had seen the remarkable demonstration of his speed with Smoke. Probably he could outdraw him, but there was always the chance that he might *not*. Instead he asked another question.

'When are you hitting the trail again?'

'When I'm good and ready.' Manning lighted his cigarette and blew the smoke languidly into Conroy's face. Conroy jerked back, half-lowered his hand to his gun, then controlled himself.

'What are you trying to be so darned tough about?' he demanded. 'Anybody here done anything to you?'

'Mebbe . . . I don't like being spied on for one thing, and I don't like being laughed at for another. Nor do I like the way things are run around here.'

Conroy turned to the gathering in the poolroom. 'You hear that, boys? City pants here doesn't like the way I run things!'

There were a couple of guffaws, but not every man in the gin palace was a cohort of Conroy. At the back a big, square-shouldered rancher with a bronzed face made a comment.

'First time somebody's had the nerve to say what a lot of us have been thinking, Conroy. *I* don't like the way things are run around here, either!'

Conroy glared. 'You'll keep your mouth shut, Big Tony, if you know what's good for you. . . .'

Manning stubbed his cigarette. 'No town,' he said, 'can prosper much if one man gives the orders and everybody else has to obey 'em because he happens to be quick on the draw. This town has possibilities if you were out of the way, and the mugs you order around.'

A short man with a pot belly, a brass watch-chain emphasizing its vulgarity, came waddling forward, a big Stetson pushed to the back of his grey-haired head. His face was dew-dropped with perspiration.

'This critter's trouble, Conroy,' he said flatly. 'Get rid of him.'

'Who the hell are you?' Manning asked pointedly.

'I'm Mayor Otis Johnson.'

'Number One Stooge, eh?' Manning suggested.

'You hear that, Conroy?' Red-faced, the Mayor swung on the saloon-owner. 'He's trying to pick a quarrel so he can use his gun. Get rid of him!'

Still Conroy hesitated – then he glanced up as another man joined the group. Tall and hatchet-faced, he looked as if he had Sioux blood in him somewhere. A star badge glittered on his chest.

'I represent the law in this town, stranger,' he said.

'Law?' Manning repeated. 'I didn't think there was any around here.'

'If there isn't I'm in the wrong job,' the sheriff said, trying not to be needled. 'There's a law in this town, same as anywhere else. I'm Sheriff Lorrimer, and it's my job to see that the mayor's wishes are carried out. You'd better go – without trouble. Else you'll be thrown – or carried – out.'

'I ain't yet heard a good reason why I should leave,' Manning said quietly.

'Because we don't trust you;' Conroy snapped. 'I reckon there's the smell of a marshal about you.'

'Yeah? Why should that bother you – unless you're up to something crooked?'

Yet another figure approached the bar, a glass of rye in his hand. Manning glanced at him with disfavour. He was fairly big, but somehow misshapen, with unusually long arms. Small eyes glittered in a narrow, lined face. His mouth was little more than a scratch. His hatless head was covered with stringy black hair plastered down in such a way as to cover the bald spots with the minimum of material.

'Get out,' he ordered, in a sharp, reedy voice. 'The mayor has absolute authority, as in any town, and if he orders you to go, you go.'

Manning ignored the request, elbows resting easily on the bar counter. 'Number Three Stooge, I assume. And quite the ugliest!'

'You're talking to Elias Marlin, attorney-at-law,' the misshapen one snapped.

Manning smiled slightly and finished off his whiskey. 'Seems the law around here must be as crooked as a corkscrew, otherwise you wouldn't look that way from studying it so much.'

There was grim laughter from various parts of the saloon, upon which Elias Marlin gave a vicious glance around him.

'Any more laughs like those and there'll be the hell of a lot of trouble.'

'You can't shoot the lot of us for laughing, Marlin,' a voice commented.

'No, but taxes can sure be stepped up plenty to make you stop holding the law in contempt.'

'Taxes?' Manning repeated. 'I figured Conroy fixed those and that the mayor carried them out. . . . Oh, I get it! You make 'em legal, so called.'

'Who's the blabbermouth been telling you so much?' the mayor demanded.

Manning did not answer. He was looking long and intently at the floor behind Marlin – which prompted Conroy to bark a question.

'What in hell are you staring at?'

'I'm looking for a trail of slime from Marlin,' Manning replied, straightening up.

Conroy whipped out his gun and held it steadily. 'That's enough, stranger! Since you don't explain your stupid insults, you'd better get out, or—'

'Sure I'll explain myself,' Manning replied, ignoring the gun. 'I came here to escape the law! Struck me as being the sort of one-eyed hole where the law would never reach – and it seems I was right.'

'Keep talking,' Conroy snapped, still holding his gun.

'That's about it – except that I object to being watched and talked about, since I'm as leery of the law catching up as you are.'

'Why?' asked Elias Marlin cynically. 'Did you steal those fancy pants, or something?' Conroy's satellites guffawed dutifully. Manning waited for the laughter to die away before replying.

'I shot two men dead because they double-crossed me. I saw clearly for the first time that human life, if it's of the trashy type, doesn't mean a thing. Might as well snuff it out.'

'Yeah,' Conroy murmured, staring. He was beginning to wonder if he had got this man wrong. 'We've been expecting a new arrival here,' he continued, 'but certainly not a killer like you. Where did you rub out those two guys?'

'Jefferson City. Since then I've been moving to keep ahead of the law.'

Conroy exchanged a quick glance with the mayor and then swung back to Manning.

'Have you been followed here?'

'That I can't say. But I know that two men have been tracking me from Jefferson City. If they ever show up I'll blot them out where they stand and bury 'em in the desert.'

'Bluff' the mayor snapped, his lips compressed.

'Mebbe I'd better introduce myself?' Manning asked, musing. 'My name's Dirk Manning. Back in Jefferson City they used to call me the 'Paleface Killer' on account of my complexion.'

'Just like a woman's,' the sheriff said tartly. 'OK, we've heard enough, and I ain't impressed. Better get moving before I forget all about laws and blast you wide open.'

Manning smiled unconcernedly. He had sensed that there were men in the pool room who were definitely on his side, and they might make plenty of trouble if there was indiscriminate shooting. He gave a quick look around him. Conroy had his gun ready, and so had the sheriff. The mayor and Elias Marlin had hardware, but were not using it. Conroy and the sheriff were standing close together. . . .

Manning acted with whirlwind speed.

From leaning on the counter he suddenly straightened and lashed out his right fist with all his power. It smashed clean into Conroy's jaw and sent him toppling backwards. Instantly the sheriff wheeled, but before he could fire Manning had landed a straight left which took the man of the law in his ample stomach. He gulped, purpled, and dropped his gun. Then he began to lurch around in gasping anguish.

Marlin fired hastily, missing by a fraction. By this time Manning had his own guns out. He fired back and the glass on the table a foot behind Marlin smashed noisily and cascaded beer over the tabletop. It dripped into Marlin's shoes as he stepped back slightly. He halted, eyes narrowed.

'Take it easy,' Manning said without emotion, as the lawyer and mayor jerked their hands up. Conroy straightened slowly and pulled the groaning, panting sheriff up beside him. They loosed their own hardware as the barrel of the left-hand .45 pinned them.

'The four of you were all set to get me, so I had to take action. Think yourselves lucky I don't drill you. But mebbe I will if you give me further cause.'

'Nice of you,' Elias Marlin spat.

'Incidentally, I've another reason for being in Macey's Folly besides hiding from the law,' Manning continued. 'I've decided, in time, to run this town in my own way. There's a good reason for that. . . .'

Manning stopped talking suddenly, looking towards the batwings. Instantly he raised his left gun and fired, twice. First one of the men at the batwings dropped, his shirt front crimsoning, and then the other fell. Men and women in the line of fire dived hastily for safety.

Manning swung round, his back to the batwings, his guns still trained on the startled four who 'ran' the town.

'Those were the two I told you about,' he said. 'Guess you'll believe me now, Mayor? They've been tailing me from Jefferson City, and evidently they caught up. Didn't do 'em much good, though! If any of you mugs have the idea that you can best me in a struggle, just take a look at those guys as a warning.'

'You saw that, Conroy?' the mayor whispered, his fat

face sweating. 'He shot 'em down without blinking! I guess even you give a guy a chance to defend himself first.' Grim silence in the saloon for a moment, then the man who had spoken in support of Manning made a move towards the bodies beside the batwings.

Manning swung one of his guns round. 'Leave 'em be, feller,' he snapped. 'Those mugs are my special meat. I'm going to take 'em out to the desert and bury 'em. Get back to where you were seated!'

Startled, the man did as he was told; then Manning added in a grim voice: 'I reckon those two men won't tail me any more. That means that in spite of anything you mugs say, I'll be back when I've disposed of their bodies.'

He continued backing away until he reached the clear space by the batwings. Then he holstered his left gun and kept his right ready. Stooping, he heaved one of the men from the floor by the shirt collar and dragged the body outside, then he pulled the other one after it. A group of the men and women who'd been watching hurried out to see what happened next. They saw Manning, still armed, heave the two men on to a horse – one of their own, presumably – and he swung to the saddle of the second one.

Then he went riding away up the main street, evidently headed for the desert to make good his threat to bury the corpses.

2

SCALPED!

It was the cynical smiles of the townsfolk at the tables that gradually made Conroy at last realize that the danger was over. 'Follow me to the office,' he said abruptly. 'This needs talking over. Andy, send in drinks.'

The barkeep, who had been transfixed throughout the proceedings, came to life.

'OK, boss.'

Five minutes later all four men, grim-faced, were seated in Conroy's office at the back of the saloon, much-needed drinks in front of them.

'This guy Manning – the Paleface Killer, as he calls himself – is dynamite,' Conroy said. 'We've never had any opposition in town like him before. If he isn't checked, it spells trouble. None of us can afford to have our affairs looked into.'

Silence. Marlin and the mayor sat scowling whilst Conroy poured himself another drink.

'We can't be *certain* he ain't a marshal, neither. Marshals ain't above disguising themselves and pulling queer tricks.'

'I don't get him as a killer,' Marlin said, frowning. 'He

looks too much of a dude.'

'Which adds up to what?' the mayor asked. 'If he is what he says – a killer on the run – he might come over to our side.'

'I don't entirely trust him,' Marlin said, musing. 'He could just be making a play to work himself in amongst us.'

'We saw him kill those two men didn't we?' the mayor demanded. 'And don't forget he took pretty good care of us in that bar skirmish. That's good enough for me. I'm inclined to believe he really is the Paleface Killer.'

'Only safe course is to have Smoke rub him out,' the sheriff said. 'We've too much at stake in this town.'

'I'd vote for that,' Marlin confirmed. All eyes then swung to Conroy. 'What do you say, Brett?'

'I just don't know.' Conroy said, rubbing his chin. 'I keep thinking about what he said – that he had *another* reason for being in town, apart from dodging the law. Only he didn't finish what he was saying. . . . What if he knows about something worthwhile in this region? Like gold, or oil? We'd be prize mugs to kill him without finding out what he knows.'

'You're crazy!' Marlin snapped. 'As a lawyer, I know every darned thing about this territory, including the parts we can take for ourselves without anybody being the wiser. There's nothing like gold or oil around here . . . in fact, Macey's Folly got its name because there *isn't* any gold! If it weren't for the fact that we make money out of the homesteaders – and the taxes they cough up – I wouldn't hang around here above five minutes!'

'No?' Conroy's eyes darkened. 'Don't ever try it, Marlin. I'm not letting you out of sight, on account of what you know—'

'Simmer down, can't you? I was speaking hypothetically,' Marlin said. 'But even if Manning did know something, you don't suppose he'd *tell* us, do you? Having Smoke take care of him is the smart thing to do, believe me.'

Abruptly Conroy made up his mind. 'You're right,' he agreed, getting to his feet. He went to the office door, opened it, and yelled for Smoke.

Within moments the red-headed gunhawk arrived. He kicked the door shut and stood waiting for orders.

'Now's your chance to get back at that big-mouthed stranger,' Conroy said, aiming a glance at him. 'We want him rubbed out – and no bungling, either.'

'With a gun?' Smoke asked.

'Of course. You can't take any chances with a guy as handy as he is.'

'Last time I wanted to rub him out, boss, you stopped me,' Smoke said, puzzled. 'You said he could be a marshal, or sump'n.'

'He isn't,' the mayor said impatiently. 'Have you forgotten how we all saw him shoot two men dead? Manning is just a trigger-happy stranger with big ideas. Just kill him, Smoke, and use as many men as you need to help you.'

Smoke looked to his boss for confirmation, got it by a nod of the head, and then left the saloon, grinning. *Carte blanche* to pump lead into the jigger who'd nearly broken his jaw had made him the happiest man alive.

But his self-conceit was such he did not call on any of the boys to help him. He felt quite sure of his own ability to deal with things. Once beyond the batwings he stood in the shadow of the boardwalk roof, out of range of the kerosene lights, and surveyed the rooming-house opposite.

A variety of twisted, sadistic thoughts passed through his mind, as he weighed up how to get Dirk Manning at his mercy. None of them involved a quick death. The ridicule to which he had been subjected when smashed over the boardwalk rail still lingered in his vindictive mind. That score had to be settled.

He realized that Manning needed to be caught unawares – so what better moment than right now, whilst he was burying the corpses in the desert? His mind made up, Smoke kicked a lounging puncher on the shin.

'Hey, you! Which way did that mug Manning go with those two bodies?'

'I dunno, but I *did* see him come back here, just a few minutes ago. He was on foot, and went into Ma Barrett's over there.' And the cowpoke inclined his head.

'Yeah?' Smoke puzzled this out. 'Mebbe he let that horse with the bodies ride where it could with 'em. Came back *walking*?' he repeated, and the cowpoke nodded.

Smoke snapped his fingers. 'I get it! Wouldn't want the horses of two dead marshals around in case they were followed. Wonder what the critter is aimin' to do next?'

The problem was answered as Manning suddenly appeared from the side of the rooming-house, astride the horse he had hired from the livery stable. He glanced about him and then hit the uptown trail at a gallop. Instantly Smoke dived down to his own horse and gave chase. Things could still fit in with his plans, as it seemed to him he would have a better chance of dealing with his quarry in the open country than in the confined regions of Ma Barrett's.

Beyond the town, Smoke rode more warily, careful not to be seen. Since Manning was almost bound to go straight ahead along the trail to the mountains, the thing to do was to get ahead of him. Pulling on the reins, Smoke sent his horse bounding up a grass bank to pasture land, then he galloped it hard through the night wind towards the point where the northward trail intersected. He gave his horse no mercy, flogging it onwards with every bit of speed he could muster.

The animal was sweating and snorting when Smoke had gained the higher ground he wanted. He dismounted and moved the horse away from direct view of the starlit trail. He dropped flat on the ground and lay watching, and listening also for the first sound of hoofbeats. At length they gradually became apparent on the night air.

The solitary figure of Manning in his light-coloured Stetson came into view, moving fast in the starlight. Smoke watched intently, realizing that the distance was too great for him to attempt using his gun ... and gradually Manning moved out of sight, still heading towards the mountains.

Smoke remounted his horse, then spurred it forward. He rode hard for ten minutes, keeping always to the higher level and promising himself he would start shooting when the lower trail – by way of a long incline – climbed up to the higher.

Now and again he drew rein and listened intently. On the third occasion he could hear the beat of hoofs from Manning's horse – which gave him all the direction he needed. There was only one way Manning could go, so Smoke went ahead, straight on into the frowning passes and mighty gorges of the mountain range, finally selecting an overhanging rock some thirty feet over the trail.

Presently the sound of Manning's horse became clearly audible and for a moment Smoke glimpsed him at the far end of the narrow pass below – then to his fury Manning turned aside into one of the clefts and disappeared. The noise of his horse ceased also and Smoke was baffled, and breathing murder.

Leaving his horse tied to a rock spur, Smoke got on the move again, gun in hand. He crept over the rocks as silently as possible, heading all the time towards the point where his quarry had disappeared. Quite unexpectedly, he came upon him in a natural hollow below. Immediately

Smoke jerked back his head and then inclined forward again, using a tall rock for cover. In puzzled interest he peered at the scene in the starlight below.

Manning was distinguishable, but the two men with whom he was conversing in low tones were only visible as the tops of hats and shoulders. Nor could Smoke pick up any of the conversation. Not far away were two horses, apparently hobbled to a mountain thicket. Smoke wondered vaguely if the men had any connection with the two he'd seen shot down. No – that was impossible.

Down below, unaware of what was happening above, Manning went on talking, the two men listening attentively.

'I think, boys, that I've managed to fool those mugs back in Macey's Folly. It hasn't been easy to make myself as objectionable as possible. Darned lucky you turned up in the saloon when you did because things were getting a bit too tight for me. I had only blanks in my left gun, but real slugs in the right – the blanks being ready for when you two showed up. When I shot the pair of you "dead" with blanks it added weight to the illusion I'd spread. . . .'

'Not much illusion about it,' one of the men broke in, grinning. 'From all accounts you're about the toughest guy who ever happened in Macey's Folly, outside of the rattlers who run it.'

Manning sighed. 'I never thought it would be so hard to act contrary to my own nature.'

'All in a good cause,' the other man said. 'How did our collapse after being "shot" look from where you were standing?'

'Perfect! That tomato ketchup in tissue-paper bags was the nearest thing to real gore I've yet seen. I thought I'd lose out when an onlooker tried to examine your bodies – but I kept him away just in time.'

'What's the next move?' the first man asked.

'Hard to say. Guess it's up to Conroy and his cronies from here on. I can't force the issue. How soon I'll need you both again I don't know. I still have the whale of a lot to do to implement my plan to. . . .'

Manning broke off, levelling his gun as a loose stone came tumbling down from above. There were split seconds of hesitation, then as he heard the sounds of scuffling footsteps he fired upwards deliberately – but uselessly.

'Somebody up there,' he snapped, leaping for his horse. 'You boys stay right here with your camp until I need you. I've got to find out how much that mug up there heard!'

Jerking his horse into action he sent it stumbling towards the nearest acclivity leading upwards. Meanwhile, Smoke was running like hell back to his own mount. That falling stone had proved his undoing – and saved Manning's life, for at that identical second Smoke's gun had been trained fully upon him.

Breathless, Smoke scrambled and ran until he gained his horse, even as he heard the sound of approaching hoof-beats from his rear. He untied it and vaulted into the saddle, his gun still in his hand, and spurred his mount forward savagely.

Moving dangerously fast on such slippery rock, he gained the point where the upper level went down in a long rubble-strewn slope to the lower trail, heading south and back to Macey's Folly. Heedless of the horse breaking a leg, Smoke spurred it onwards relentlessly, dust rising in clouds under the thundering hoofs.

But the sound of pursuit deepened, chiefly because Smoke's horse was almost exhausted from its earlier efforts, whereas Manning's was not.

'Faster, damn you!' Smoke panted, jamming his spurred heels into the horse's flanks. But all his cruel efforts were useless. The beast had reached the limit of its strength and its speed slowed alarmingly. Smoke swore luridly and hipped round in his saddle, aiming his gun in the starlight at his pursuer. Smoke fired, but his shot went wide – and one in return also went wide. Their horses' jolting made steady aim impossible, and the starlight and drifting dust didn't help.

Suddenly Smoke threw his leg from the saddle and leapt to the ground. Scrambling up on to one knee he tried to take careful aim.

Before Smoke could fire a bullet whanged so close beside his ear he thought it had struck him. He was thrown off his mark by the shock, and the next thing he knew Manning had jumped from his horse and was coming forward, his gun covering him relentlessly.

'Get up!' Manning ordered. Smoke obeyed slowly. His gun was snatched from his hand and the remaining one from its holster.

'My old friend with the carroty hair!' Manning gave a dry chuckle as he recognized the other. 'What were you doing back there in the foothills?'

'I could ask you the same question!'

'You were probably spying for that hoodlum Brett Conroy. What did you see, or hear?'

'I heard nothin',' Smoke responded sullenly. 'How in hell could I at that distance? And all I saw was two blasted hats and two pairs of shoulders.'

'I wish I could believe that.' Manning muttered.

'It's true, I tell you! I didn't hear nothin'. An' if you're goin' to plug me, just get on with it.'

Manning shook his head in the gloom. He was more or less satisfied that Smoke had spoken the truth. The distance had been too great to hear anything, and it was unlikely he could have recognized the faces of the two men who had been "shot" in the Swaying Hip.

'I'm not killing you,' he said levelly. 'I want you to take a message back to that big-shot boss of yours, just to show him – and you – that you ain't so smart.'

'Message?' Smoke repeated blankly. 'What in hell kind of message?'

Instead of answering, Manning clicked his teeth and his horse loped forward. Still holding his gun, he reached out his free hand and took down a lariat from the saddle horn. Deftly he dropped the rope end into a slipknot and formed a noose. Since he was still covered by the gun there was nothing Smoke could do as the noose dropped squarely over his shoulders and pinned his arms to his sides.

Manning dropped his .45 back into its holster and proceeded to tie the gunman up so securely that Smoke could scarcely move hand or foot.

'What's the idea – a rough ride back to Macey's Folly?' Smoke demanded hoarsely.

'It's an idea – and right up your street. But I've other notions. You need something to remember me by. More ways of making a man of your type smart than just killing you. I figure you for a conceited oaf, Smoke. You're proud of the fact that you can kill, that you have a mop of red hair. . . .'

'You ain't makin' any sense,' Smoke growled.

'Let me finish! I aim to make you the laughing stock of Macey's Folly. If you've any women in tow – and I don't doubt you have – of the same type as yourself they'll prefer in future to have nothing to do with you!'

'Stop talking rubbish, can't you?' There was uneasiness, even fear, in Smoke's tone because he was unsure of what was coming. 'Spit out what you're really driving at. . . .'

'Be easier to demonstrate.' Manning thrust out his hand and pushed Smoke flat on his back, with a jar that shook his back teeth. Then, kneeling beside him,

36

Manning took out his jackknife. With his free hand he grasped Smoke's hat and hurled it to the winds, then he grabbed a handful of the exposed red hair.

Smoke's hair was being cut steadily, without mercy, great clumps of it down to the roots. Manning worked ruthlessly, throwing handfuls of hair away and then continuing to hack until he was down to the very scalp.

'You swine!' Smoke screamed. 'You dirty swine—' Smoke writhed and twisted and then shrieked as he felt the blade cut into his scalp, as he was held down in a relentless grip.

'Keep your damned head still if you don't want your scalp gouging,' Manning said implacably. Smoke came as near to weeping as he had ever done in his adult life. His flaming red hair was his one pride. His front quiff vanished with one slash of the blade.

Manning was unrelenting, one knee on Smoke's chest and one hand pinning down the shifting head. At length there was only a bristly mat left on the gunman's head with the white of his scalp below.

'You can be thankful I'm not a redskin,' Manning said drily, standing up and snapping his jackknife shut. 'Better change your name from 'Smoke' to 'Baldy' from now on. And if you ever come after me again I'll cut your throat instead of your hair. This is an advance warning.'

'You won't get the chance – I'll kill you for this!' Smoke yelled frantically.

Manning merely smiled grimly as he reached down and hauled the gunman to his bound feet, catching him over one broad shoulder as he toppled forward. Smoke was carried a few yards and dumped sideways on to his horse. With his own lariat Manning tied him into position, then stood back.

'Up to you whether this cayuse ever gets to Macey's Folly,' he said. 'You can still yell directions even if you can't use the reins.' With that, Manning suddenly delivered a sharp slap on the horse's flanks. Instantly the horse, now somewhat recovered, got on the move.

For a while, Smoke's lurid ravings were carried back on the night air. Unarmed, trussed like a steer about to be branded, and his head like a gooseberry he was at this moment incandescent with fury. . . . Then the horse carried him out of earshot and Manning relaxed. He turned back to where he had left his own horse.

He swung into the saddle and headed back to his friends' camp in the foothills, where they were waiting anxiously, armed and on the alert. Recognizing him, they holstered their weapons.

'Well, who was it?' one of men asked.

Dismounting, Manning rapidly gave them the details.

'I packed him off back to Macey's Folly,' he finished, 'but since he's Conroy's right-hand man, he may send his gang snooping around here before long. Better move higher up the mountains where you can watch what happens. Plenty of caves up there.'

Manning's two friends glanced at one another in the starlight and grinned. Then one of them asked a question:

'So what's next? Seems to me that if you ride back into town you'll run smack into Conroy and his boys. They'll be gunning for you after this night's work on that guy Smoke.'

'You're right,' Manning assented. 'I'm not risking it tonight, anyways. I'll stay with you guys, then I can see where the camp is going to be shifted for when I need you again. Come on, sooner we move, the better.'

By dint of barking directions from time to time, Smoke had eventually succeeded in getting his horse to return him to Macey's Folly. Now it was slowly loping along the main street, and, within minutes, Smoke was discovered by the men beginning to leave the Swaying Hip.

As he was unfastened, the first laughs came, deepening into guffaws. One man called another, and in the end a dozen or so yelling cowpokes were staring at Smoke or pointing to his ravaged head.

'Have your laughs, damn you!' Smoke yelled back at them, grabbing the hat of the nearest man and jamming it on his own head. 'When I get my hands on some hardware, I'll blast you grinning hyenas wide open!'

The men only laughed all the more, so, swearing blue murder, Smoke strode into the saloon. His agitated speed proved his undoing as the sudden gust of air through the batwings as he crashed between them whipped the over-large hat from his head.

Bleak fury on his ugly face, he stood there with a hand on his bald dome. The punchers still lingering over their drinks before closing time glanced up, and then a great howl went up as the mortified arrival was identified.

'Hell, Smoke, that sure is one man-sized haircut you got there!'

'Bin a forest fire on your skull, feller?'

'Shut up!' Smoke roared. 'You don't think I got this of me own free will, do yuh?'

Conroy strolled over from the bar counter, grinning round his cheroot. 'So what happened?' he asked. 'You're bald as an egg and covered in trail dust.'

'That guy Dirk Manning did it. The Paleface Killer, as he calls himself. Soon as I see him again, I'll drill him.'

'You've said that before,' Conroy said in contempt. 'Every time I turn you loose to deal with that blabber-mouth you get yourself hogtied. And from the looks of things he took your hardware as well.'

'Sure he did – but you can get fresh guns for me, boss. An' you lot can stop grinnin'!' Smoke spat, turning to the men and women around him. 'I just couldn't stop that bastard peelin' me hair off.'

'Better give him a drink, Andy,' Conroy said, signalling to the barkeep. 'Looks like he needs one.'

It was brought over as Conroy waved the gawping crowd aside, then jerked his head to the mayor, sheriff, and finally Elias Marlin. They followed as he led the way to his office. Receiving the signal, the bald-headed Smoke went there too, clutching his half-finished drink.

'Some mug you are,' Sheriff Lorrimer commented sourly. 'Mebbe you've outlived your usefulness around here.' He half-drew his gun, then checked as Conroy grabbed his arm.

'Forget the hardware, Sheriff' he ordered. 'It's not Smoke we've got a beef against: it's this guy Manning. Something's got to be done – an' quick.'

'I'm surprised,' Marlin said, thinking, 'that Manning didn't put a slug through Smoke here instead of giving him a much-needed haircut.'

'The guy wouldn't shoot me!' Smoke said, glaring. 'I wish he had – I reckon I'd sooner be a stiff than lookin' like this.'

'Tell us exactly what happened,' Conroy said impatiently.

'I followed the critter from here to the foothills. . . .' And Smoke gave the whole story, with embellishments on how he had tried to defend himself, and exonerating himself from blame for the misfortune of the loose stone giving him away, just as he was drawing a bead.

The other men were grimly silent and Smoke looked from one to the other uneasily. Marlin, in particular, was unimpressed by the account.

'Judging by that performance, you'll never get near to Manning. And I still think that you've become a liability – a gunman who can't do his job.'

'I'll make the decisions around here,' Conroy said. He

glanced at Smoke. 'Why the hell didn't you take some of the boys with you? You could easily have dealt with Manning then – and the men with him. I told you to get the boys – or at least, the mayor did.'

'I figured I could work best by myself.' Smoke put down his now empty glass, and drew the back of his hand over his mouth. 'Let me have two more guns, boss, an' I'll—'

'You didn't see these two men he was talking to?' Conroy interrupted, thinking.

'Nope. I was too high up. I couldn't hear 'em either.'

'Sounds to me as though he might be an outlaw on the run at that,' Elias Marlin mused. 'Mebbe he and two pard-ners of his are hiding out. Doesn't sound as if he's a marshal or anything connected with the authorities.'

'Which makes it we can rub him out more openly.' the sheriff pointed out.

Conroy nodded absently. 'If only I could figure out what he really *wants*!' he muttered, beating a fist on his knee. 'If he's not a law officer, then it isn't us he's after. And if he's a killer as he makes out, he wouldn't be mug enough to stop long in one town, not when those marshals got near enough to find him. I know he said he wants to run Macey's Folly the way he likes it, but I reckon that was only talk. The only explanation is that he's got something mighty important in mind for this district. He knows some secret that we don't.'

Silence again. Then Smoke said: 'Get every manjack in the region and set about finding him. Blast him out!'

'But if we kill him,' Marlin mused, 'we may spoil things for ourselves – just like you said we would earlier, Conroy. Since we've already tried and failed once, it might be smarter after all to wait and see what he does next. He may lead us to something big – then we'll deal with him.'

'About time you saw it my way,' Conroy growled. 'So we're all agreed?'

'I still think we should find him and blast hell outa him,' Smoke said. 'I'll act on my own if needs be. No guy's goin' to get away with what he did to me!'

Conroy aimed a sharp glance. 'You'll do as you're told, Smoke – not as you like. Step out of line and you'll be eliminated. Your hair will grow again,' he added drily, getting to his feet. 'Probably the lice on your scalp need to see the daylight, anyhow.'

3

LASH OF THE WHIP

Manning was awake at sun-up, shaved with the solitary razor the boys carried with them, and then had a breakfast of the inevitable canned beans, bread and coffee.

'Figuring on ridin' back into town?' one of the men asked.

'Later in the day, mebbe. My first call this morning is the Double Triangle ranch. Like I told you last night, I don't get the idea of that guy Haslam running it. He shouldn't be there, as you know, so there must be something dodgy back of it. . . . When I've had a look around there I'll take my chance in the town.'

'Like as not they'll be waiting for you,' said the second man seriously.

'Could be,' Manning shrugged, 'but all three of us were ready for trouble when we took this job. I guess that the three hundred thousand dollars we're hoping to split three ways isn't going to come without risks.' He got to his feet and glanced about him.

'Things seem quiet enough, so I'll get moving. Stay right here and keep out of sight if anybody comes snooping. Don't shoot unless you're forced to – and you can

43

keep those guns of Smoke's. Hardware's always useful.'

He filled his water bottle from the barrel and fixed it on his saddle with a small pack of provisions. Then he swung on to his horse. The other two men waved as he rode out.

He rode cautiously on the downward trail, alert for the first sign of a daylight investigation by Conroy or his men, but there were no signs of anybody. So, his vigilance somewhat relaxed, he rode northwards in the general direction of the Double Triangle ranch, a five-mile journey.

He looked appreciatively around him on his leisurely ride, gazing upon the golden fields of brittle-bush and beyond them to the infinite blue spaces of the mesa where cobalt sky and desert met in misty union. He picked out orange mariposa tulips swaying in the hot wind, amidst the lilac-tinted carpets of wild verbena and purple hyptis. It was hard to believe that arid desert lay beyond those myriads of yuccas – the Lord's Candles – with their eight-foot-high shafts of creamy bloom.

The hot, exhilarating Arizona morning momentarily took his mind off what lay behind his mission in Macey's Folly. He smiled to himself as he rode steadily north, and overhead in the cloudless sky swifts darted with incredible agility.

Manning slowed as the Double Triangle ranch came into view, finally drawing to a halt on a high, level stretch from where he could survey the spread. It was big, with its 5,000 head of cattle grazing in the sunlight, having vacated their large corrals. The men of the ranch outfit were working around the barns and stables, and in the corrals themselves. For a time the solitary figure against the blue sky remained watching – then with the old inflexible look coming back to his powerful face he began to descend the slope.

Reaching the outermost fence he neck-reined his horse, and began a slow circuit of the ranch, surveying it from every angle. The men at work paused and looked at him in surprise – but they did not challenge him. As long as he kept beyond the spread's limits there was no law to stop him gazing.

On his second circuit, he paused to study the big ranch house with its massive chimney-breasts jutting from the seasoned wood roof. There were the usual rear and front porches, screen doors, shutters to put across the windows – open at the moment – and also the. . . .

'What do you think you're doing, stranger?'

Looking up, Manning found himself facing a girl. She sat on the top rail of the fence, the heels of her half-boots locked on the lower rail. She wore blue Levis and a white blouse with the sleeves rolled up on comfortably plump arms. Possibly she was twenty-three, with a wealth of chestnut-coloured hair. As he jogged nearer, he noticed she had greyish-brown eyes – and a rifle in her hands.

'Just looking. Do you mind?'

'Of course I do! This place isn't a peepshow!'

'I was just admiring this mighty fine ranch – I didn't mean to get on your nerves.'

As the girl looked at Manning fixedly, he noticed that she was fairly good-looking except for a too-short nose. Her exposed skin was burned a delicate reddish brown tint, making him slightly self-conscious about his own town-bred lack of colour.

'You'd better be on your way,' she said eventually. 'Strangers aren't welcome around here. I'm asking you to leave nicely. If my stepfather should see you he won't be nearly as gentle, and is even liable to put a bullet through you.'

'You talking about Nat Haslam?' Manning asked. The girl looked surprised.

'Oh, so you know our name? Yes – Nat Haslam is my stepfather.'

The girl climbed down on Manning's side and propped her rifle against the fence, having decided that she would not have to use it. She gave Manning a puzzled look.

'How come you know so much about us? I've never even seen you before.'

'I only arrived here yesterday. The name's Dirk Manning, sometimes known as the Paleface Killer.'

'Is that killer tag supposed to make me swoon in horror?'

'Not at all. I've never harmed a woman in my life – but I have killed men, and probably shall again.'

The girl frowned, still puzzled. Then she shrugged plump shoulders. 'I still say you'd better go – and quickly.'

Manning kept his horse motionless in the hot sun. 'I know your stepfather's name, but I don't know yours.'

'It's Tracey Lee – if that's any business of yours. My mother is dead, and obviously my father is.' The girl looked moodily in front of her after she'd spoken, her mouth pursed into an expression that hinted at self-pity. Then she added: 'Look, mister, for your own good, get going! If my stepfather should— Oh!' she broke off with a startled gasp.

Manning followed her alarmed gaze across the big yard, to where a heavily built man of middle age was rapidly approaching. He was hatless, dressed in flannel shirt and riding-pants, his half-boots caked with refuse from the stable floors. The sun beat down on a square head with close-cropped grey hair. No gun was in evidence, but in one hand he was carrying a short stock-whip.

Manning saw that he was a leathery-brown man with harshly cut, sour face. Three feet from the fence he paused and glared up at him with close-set blue eyes.

'What the hell d'yuh think you're doing, hanging around and talkin' to Tracey here?' he demanded. 'I ain't havin' my daughter talkin' to strangers!'

'Stepdaughter, don't you mean?'

'Who in hell are you to sort out my family?'

'Like I told your stepdaughter – I'm just looking.'

'Better look some place else – fast! As for you, Tracey, git back on your own side of the fence. You oughta have more sense than have truck with strangers.'

'No harm in talking, Pa,' the girl answered, shrugging 'I get precious little chance to speak to anybody around here. You don't have to get so awkward about it.'

'Awkward?' Haslam repeated, his mouth setting venomously. 'You talking to *me*, gal?'

Tracey did not answer. She looked frightened, but she held her ground.

'Surely she's old enough to say what she thinks?' Manning said mildly.

'I'll fix you, stranger,' Haslam breathed. 'Git back over here, gal – and quick!'

The girl gave a bitter glance, then prepared to climb over to her own territory.

'That the way you always talk to your stepdaughter?' Manning asked. 'I'm not sure I like it.'

'Who the hell asked you? Git going afore I lays this whip about your shoulders!'

As Manning hesitated, Tracey had obeyed the order and scrambled back over the fence. She had hardly done so before she gave a gasp of pain as the tails of the short, vicious whip slashed across her back. The flimsy blouse immediately became defiled with thin red lines.

'I'll teach yuh to lip me, gal!' her stepfather shouted. 'Git back in the house and keep—'

He got no further before Manning exploded into action. In a single movement, he swung his leg over the saddle, dropped, then vaulted the fence and seized the older man's wrist. With a savage twist he tore the whip

47

from him and flung it far beyond the fence into the open pasture.

'Seems to me,' Dirk Manning said, 'you're one of those roughneck cowards who like to beat on helpless women. Try handling me and see how you like it.'

'You blasted, interfering scum!' The girl's stepfather lashed out a fist, but it failed to land and instead he received a haymaker under the chin, which flung him backwards to the baked earth. As he tried to rise, another bone-snapping uppercut belted him backwards again. He stumbled on his heels, tripped, and dropped half into the nearby horse trough.

'For heaven's sake, go!' the girl panted, gripping Manning's arm. 'He'll bring the rest of the boys to deal with you, and they'll. . . .'

As the swearing, dripping Haslam tried to emerge from the trough, Manning contemptuously thrust out his hand and immersed him fully into the trough again. He spluttered in anguish as the water surged over him.

'Sorry, Miss Tracey,' Manning said. 'Guess I don't like kicking around an older man, but this time I think it's justified. You have any more trouble with this brute, come straight into town and ask for me – Dirk Manning. I'll protect you.'

The girl stood bewildered, looking from one man to the other. Manning gave her an encouraging smile. It faded as he noticed her flayed back, and that in the distance a bunch of men were running towards them. He couldn't possibly deal with so many of them.

'Better get that back fixed,' he said. 'Meantime I must be going. Look me up sometime in town.' Swiftly he returned to his horse, swinging to the saddle. In a moment he had spurred it quickly away.

He kept on riding steadily, half-expecting to be pursued, but nothing happened. At length he came upon the trail leading directly into Macey's Folly.

Here he slowed down, ready for trouble. All seemed quiet in the town, however, and he saw no men especially watching for him. In fact there were more women than men around, busy shopping and generally going forth about the morning's business. This early the majority of the men would be at work on the outlying spreads.

Manning rode on until he came to an office, the window of which carried the inscription: ELIAS MARLIN, ATTORNEY-AT-LAW. Here he dismounted, tied his horse to the hitch rail, then strode into the lawyer's office.

Marlin himself was at a roll-top desk, most of it hidden by deeds and sheets of parchment. He turned in the swivel-chair at the sound of his visitor. His small eyes narrowed, and the scar of a mouth nearly disappeared as he compressed his lips.

'What do you want?' he snapped. 'Ain't you got more sense than to come riding into town again like this?'

'Listen, Marlin: I do what I like. As for what I want – it's information.'

Manning half-perched on the nearby table, pushing aside deeds to make room for his thigh. Marlin's hand lowered casually to his gun and then jumped up again as his visitor's own .45 leapt into his fingers.

'Don't try it,' Manning advised, his voice level. 'I've a weakness for shooting snakes.'

Marlin glanced about him, realized that he was trapped.

'All right, I'm listening.'

'I'm here to talk about the Double Triangle.' Marlin's expression changed slightly, but he was schooled enough in the art of concealing his emotions not to give anything away.

49

'How come that spread interests you?'

'The reason doesn't signify. What *does* is that there's a leather-necked swine running it who thinks nothing of flaying his stepdaughter with a stock-whip.'

'You laying a legal complaint against Haslam?' Marlin asked drily.

'No – I've already soaked his thick head in a horse trough to cool him down.'

'Damnit, Manning, are you loco?' Marlin exclaimed. 'Why rile every dangerous man in town? Haslam's plenty mean and will be on the prod for you from here on.'

'The skunks around here don't worry me any,' Manning returned sourly. 'Even the crafty ones like you. What I want to know is: what is Haslam doing running the Double Triangle? When did he take it over?'

'I'm a lawyer, Manning. I can't discuss my clients with you. Now get out.'

Manning looked thoughtful, his gun steady in his hand. Marlin realized he'd given more away than he intended by referring to Haslam as his client.

'I happen to know that ranch belonged to Clint Dawson,' Manning said thinly. 'And when he died the spread should have been left empty. Why wasn't it?' He leaned forward suddenly, emphasizing his question by pressing the muzzle of his .45 against Marlin's pigeon chest.

'There's some crooked business about that ranch,' Manning added. 'That polecat Haslam has no right to be there – or any of the others either, including his step-daughter Tracey.'

'So you know all about them, do you?' Marlin let out his breath as Manning lifted his gun off his chest, but kept it levelled. 'What's your interest in the Double Triangle, anyway?'

'I happen to know those folks are there illegally and I'll give you just forty-eight hours to get them out.'

Marlin stared in genuine amazement. 'You can't give me orders like that, Manning! Haslam is in the Double Triangle by grant of a legal deed, and he'll go on being there. He—'

'Clint Dawson left no such orders and he owned that ranch. It was left empty to stay empty. I know because I've seen his will.'

'How? Nobody but a lawyer's supposed to see a will, and you sure are not one.'

'It ain't necessary to be a lawyer to see a will. You should brush the dust off your legal tomes. The will was lodged with Alderton Dodd, one of Jefferson City's biggest lawyers. If you haven't heard of it you should because it can make you empty that ranch pronto. I discovered that before I rode out to here. I'd have been here sooner only I was in jail.'

Marlin looked over to the pile of papers on top of his safe, then, disregarding the gun, he got to his feet and went over to them. As Manning watched him closely, gun in hand, he found what he wanted, a thick foolscap document folded in three. Marlin came back to his desk.

'Take a look at that,' he said, and handed the deed over.

Manning shook the document open, reading it in glances whilst he kept the wily lawyer covered. Ostensibly the paper was the will of Clint Dawson, duly witnessed by Marlin himself, and bequeathing all his property and personal possessions to the township of Macey's Folly to be disposed of as the authority of the town should see fit.

'Satisfied?' Marlin asked with a cynical grin. 'We have there Clint Dawson's absolute permission to do as we wish with his ranch – and what *was* done with it isn't your business!'

Manning was silent for several moments, gazing into

distance and toying with the gun in his hand. Then he threw the will back on the desk in contempt.

'This will's a fake, Marlin – like you! Where's the real will?'

'That *is* the real one.' Marlin squirmed in his seat. 'The only will Dawson left! What more do you want?'

'You're lying! As a lawyer you'll know that all wills made west of Jefferson City have to be recorded in Jefferson City archives as *well as* in the actual town where the will is made. That's the law.'

'I never heard of a law about Jefferson City having to have duplicate—'

'You're lying. It's clear to me now that the real will was torn up and this one faked in its place. You never expected anybody to turn up and challenge it. I repeat what I've said – you have forty-eight hours to throw out Haslam and those with him.'

'Just why are you so concerned about getting that ranch emptied?' Marlin demanded. 'Are you working for the Jefferson City authorities?'

'I happen to be interested in protecting the late Clint Dawson's property. He was a friend of mine. Whose idea was it to put Haslam in, anyhow?'

'Brett Conroy's.' Marlin realized he was cornered and must therefore shift the blame. 'Everything that happens around here, crooked or otherwise, is his doing.'

'So what kind of a heel does that make you, working for him?'

Marlin grinned sourly. 'A self-admitted killer having the gall to preach honesty!'

'There can be such a thing as an honest killer. Very different from the slimy twisting of the law which you practise.' Manning holstered his gun and then stood up.

'I'll expect them out of that ranch in two days, or I'll

throw 'em out myself. And I'll find out why Conroy put them there.'

With that Manning left, slamming the office door behind him. Instantly, Marlin moved to the window and peered outside. He watched as Manning paused on the boardwalk, seemingly thinking something out. Then he stepped down to his horse, mounted it, and rode out of town.

Marlin hurried to the rear of his office building, where his own horse was stabled. He also rode out of town, branching off when he had covered perhaps a mile and cutting across pastures and grazing land. Presently he had arrived at the Blazing C, Conroy's own prosperous spread.

A cheroot smouldering between his teeth, Conroy was busy counting a pile of money in the living-room of the ranch house when Marlin was shown into the room. He looked up hastily, then deftly swept the money into the desk drawer and glared at his visitor.

'What is it, Marlin? I'm busy. You're none too welcome at this time of day.'

'Mebbe I'm not welcome at any time of day,' the lawyer commented, his eyes straying to the drawer into which the money had been swept. 'But this is important. I didn't trail this far in the heat for fun.' He sat down and fanned himself with his hat. 'Dirk Manning has come back to town.'

'So what? We agreed that we leave him be, remember? It was your own suggestion. Time enough to bother me when something happens.'

'Mebbe it already has. Manning came to my office and forced me to talk on the wrong end of the hardware. For some reason I can't figure he's told me to get the Double Triangle spread vacated within forty-eight hours or else!'

'What!' Conroy snatched out his cheroot. 'Who the hell does he think he is? A lawyer?'

'He's no lawyer, Brett, though he's certainly got an

unhealthy grasp of legal matters. Says he is an old friend of Clint Dawson. Mebbe he's that guy we were watching for, but he's arrived in such an unusual way that we're caught on the hop.'

'Could be,' Conroy muttered, returning his cheroot to his mouth and chewing it savagely. 'Did he say anything else?'

'Not much. I have to empty the Double Triangle or he'll do it for me. He's even seen the original will in Jefferson City . . . Remember I *told* you someone might get on to us, but you wouldn't listen.'

'Quit whining!' Conroy got to his feet, pacing round the big room before turning to face the misshapen lawyer directly. 'How much does Manning actually *know?*'

'He certainly knows the will is a forgery. Naturally I didn't admit to him that I know Jefferson City has a duplicate of the real one. He also knows Haslam has no legal right to the Double Triangle.'

'He's staying right where I put him. If necessary, I can get the boys together and blast Manning wide open. To hell with his secret knowledge! He's now too dangerous to have around.'

Marlin was doing some hard thinking. 'Since we know Clint Dawson left everything to his nephew Mark Dawson we—' The lawyer stopped. He could see from the look on Conroy's face he had thought of the same thing.

'That's who he is!' he cried. 'Mark Dawson, nephew of old Clint! That's why he means to stick around. The very guy we were watching for, but when he didn't show up we figured we were safe.'

'He would have came earlier only he's been in jail. So he said.'

'So that's the reason? Damnit, he's tougher than old Clint himself, and he was terror enough. So he's blown in to claim his ranch – belatedly – found it's been already taken over and now has given you, Marlin, two days to empty the place.'

'But what about that line he handed us about being the 'Paleface Killer' on the run for a killing?'

'Just talk,' Conroy sneered. 'Trying to make himself look hard and throw a scare into us.'

'I get the idea that he *is* hard,' Marlin said morosely. 'We banked on a lilywhite who'd do just as he was told. Old Clint himself used to say his nephew was just a timid city kid . . . And look how he turned out! In the interval while old man Dawson never saw him he's turned into a real hardcase.'

'Not so hard he can't be broken,' Conroy growled. 'In a straight gunfight I'd blow him away. He's not getting his hands on the Double Triangle, either. That spread's a mighty valuable one and those cattle turn in the hell of a lot of money.'

'So you're rubbing him out?'

'Tonight. You and me and the boys'll go over to Ma Barrett's and have things out with him before we kill him. If he ain't there we'll soon find him.'

Marlin didn't say anything. Instead he just sat brooding. Conroy stopped his pacing and glared at the lawyer.

'You gone to sleep, Marlin?' he demanded testily.

Marlin stirred. 'Young Dawson is about the most dangerous man we've ever tackled. Since we're agreed he should be rubbed out I think it should be done instantly, and no monkeying around.'

'We still need to find out first if he really is Dawson's nephew,' Conroy said, walking over to the window. 'We don't want to have to deal with the real nephew later. That's why I had you fix the faked will – in case the nephew showed up.'

Marlin smiled bitterly. 'And that guy threw it back in my face. He isn't a fool, Brett, and we'd do best to remember it.'

'I will. OK, you can leave it to me to fix it up with the rest of the boys. We'll meet tonight in the Swaying Hip and go over to Ma Barrett's in a body. Time there was another shooting on her premises anyway.'

4

ROUGH HOUSE

On leaving town, Mark Dawson – alias Manning – rode without halt to the foothills, and eventually to the cave hideout of his two friends. Alert for any intruders, they put away their guns when they recognized him.

'Back in time for lunch?' one of them said with a grin. 'Or did you run into trouble?'

'Not yet – but I'm likely to.' Manning came over from his horse and joined them where a meal had been laid out. 'I've been to the Double Triangle, and found it's being run by a sadistic louse named Haslam. He's probably in cahoots with Conroy, and the pair of them – with the bright boys who run Macey's Folly thrown in – are creaming off a handsome profit from it. I've given the shyster lawyer behind it forty-eight hours to get the ranch empty.'

The other man looked dubious. 'Does he know you're Dawson's nephew Mark?'

'I didn't tell him, but he may soon tumble to it since I'm the only beneficiary under the original will. Of course that's only half the story why we're here.' Mark's two comrades nodded slowly, going on eating their beans.

'I'm not confident my ultimatum will be met,' Mark

continued. 'They'll almost certainly try to get rid of me now, as the one person standing in their way. I'm prepared for that, but emptying the ranch is going to pose a real problem.'

'Why should it?' the shorter man asked. 'Cliff and I will help you do it – unless you're worried about us being seen returning to life?'

'No, Harry.' Mark shook his head. 'Conroy's probably realized by now I'm not the killer I pretended to be.' He hesitated. 'It's a girl by the name of Tracey Lee. She's Haslam's stepdaughter and as pretty as a sunset. If I start trouble at the Double Triangle she'll get caught up in it, and that's the last thing I want to risk. She's as sweet and straight as her stockwhip-wielding stepfather is cruel and crooked.'

'Well,' Harry observed, chewing slowly, 'the only answer is to get the gal away from the spread *before* the lead starts flying around.'

'Thanks for seeing it my way.' Mark smiled ruefully. 'I was afraid you'd think I'd gone soft or something.'

'You *have*,' Harry replied frankly. 'Any guy who lets a woman cloud his judgement is nuts – but I guess we all succumb to it eventually.'

'I wonder,' Cliff asked presently, 'if that smart shyster lawyer has figured out all the dope concerning that three hundred thousand dollars?'

Mark shook his head. 'Unlikely. My uncle left that to me as separate from his will – a private letter, which only I and Alderton Dodd have seen. That's why we're in this tangle right now.'

'It's odd,' Harry reflected, 'the queer wills folk make sometimes.'

'We've *got* to get the girl clear.' Mark's thoughts were already elsewhere. 'I can't ask her to leave the ranch with me because Haslam will be waiting to shoot me on sight.

So you've gotten yourself a job, Harry.'

'A job? Doing what?'

'Keep an eye on the Double Triangle and report to me the moment Tracey gets on the move – as she must do at some time or other. Will you do it?'

'Sure!' Harry shrugged. 'Where will I report to you? Here?'

'No. I'm going back into town.' Then seeing their expressions Mark added: 'I'm not loco, boys. I need to keep an eye on Conroy and his men. I'm gambling that when they see I'm not leery of them, they'll hesitate before attacking me.'

'They might in any case.' Cliff commented soberly. 'I don't like it, Mark.'

'I'm risking it anyway – soon as I've finished this chow. When anything turns up regarding the girl, Harry, you'll find me at Ma Barrett's rooming-house.'

His companions nodded. Getting their hands on $300,000 was a powerful incentive to take risks.

The meal over, Mark rode part of the way back to Macey's Folly with Harry beside him, leaving Cliff to guard the cave hideout. A mile outside the town Harry turned off across open country towards the Double Triangle whilst Mark rode on into town.

He was fully alert for trouble when he arrived, but none came. There were few people about in the drowsy early afternoon heat, and those on the boardwalks ignored him. He left his horse in Ma Barrett's stable, entered the establishment and went up to his room. Cautiously he peered through the lace curtains of the window on to the main street, but saw nothing suspicious.

But Elias Marlin, from his office, had seen him come into town and the fact was soon communicated to Conroy in his office back of the saloon. Immediately he began to lay his plans to strike at the safest time – after nightfall.

Conroy was fairly sure that even Dawson wouldn't risk coming into the Swaying Hip during the evening.

Nor did he. He was instead quietly thinking out his next move. He had to empty the Double Triangle for one thing, and for another he had to implement his reason for being in town. After the evening meal around seven he went back to his room, rolled and lit a cigarette, relaxing as he thought things through.

And across the road, imperceptibly, one by one Conroy's satellites began to arrive – until by sundown they had all gathered in his office. Joining Conroy were the pot-bellied mayor, hatchet-faced sheriff, bald-headed Smoke, misshapen Marlin, and about half a dozen strong-arm boys.

'He's still in town, boss,' one of them reported. 'I've been watching from a spot where he couldn't see me from his window. He ain't left that rooming-house and his cayuse is still in the stable.'

'That's right enough,' another man confirmed. 'I've been watching as well – from the opposite end of the street. Nothing's happened.'

'It will soon.' Conroy smiled grimly. 'Whether or not he tells us what we want to know, we're going to finish him tonight.' He glanced at the clock. 'Give it another hour and then we'll move. Len – Shorty, get outside again and keep the joint cased.'

Len and Shorty departed and for the next hour Conroy and his boys spent their time in the saloon, drinking and yarning – then when the time was up they met on the boardwalk outside, where they were joined by Len and Shorty. Then they moved quickly across the street. The yellow square of a lighted upper-room window over the slope-roofed porchway showed in the darkness.

Reaching the rooming-house, Conroy strode into the hall, then straight through it and into the kitchen regions.

Ma Barrett and her husband, just at the close of washing up crockery, turned in surprise.

'What the hell do you mean by bustin' in here?' old man Barrett demanded, limping forward.

'Hold it, old-timer!' Conroy snarled. 'Unless you want my slug in that other leg of yours? I want to know if that guy Dirk Manning is in his room.'

'Why do you want to know that?' Ma Barrett snapped, and as Conroy turned to the woman, her husband slipped through the door, presumably to give a warning call above. The cry died stillborn on his lips as he found himself looking at grim-faced men in the hallway, two of them with their guns cocked and pointed directly at him.

'Thanks,' Conroy said drily, seizing the old man by the shoulder and hurling him aside. 'So he *is* up there. Steve, stay right here and watch these two. The rest of you follow me upstairs – quietly as possible.'

He paused at the topmost step. The faint glow of a landing light had not sufficient power to blot out the line of illumination under the door that lay over the hall and the front of the house. Conroy grinned, tightened his hold on his gun, then glided forward. Outside the door he stopped, listening intently. Silence.

Inside the room, Mark was sitting in the chair at the table, the chair on its hind legs and he with his heels on the table's corner. Completely relaxed, he was rolling a cigarette.

Which gave Conroy the complete advantage. With one terrific kick he slammed the door back and stood on the threshold with his gun ready. Mark dropped the makings and reacted quickly, his right-hand .45 flashing into his fingers – only to be blown out of them again by a bullet from Conroy's gun.

The initiative clearly lost, Mark sat nursing his tingling but otherwise undamaged fingers and smiled bitterly.

'What happens now, or shouldn't I ask?'

'Get his other gun, Smoke,' Conroy ordered. He came further into the room. As Smoke moved forward Mark eyed him in dour amusement.

'Not found any hair-restorer yet?' he murmured, and was rewarded by a stinging slap in the face. He showed no reaction as he contemplated the other men who had piled into the little room. 'Surely it doesn't take an entire mob of hyenas like this to pay off for Smoke's haircut?'

'This ain't about Smoke's haircut,' Conroy said levelly. 'Marlin here tells me you've uncommon interest in the Double Triangle. I want to know *why*.'

'I've a question myself,' Mark said. 'Have you got Haslam and the rest of them out of the Double Triangle yet? If not, why not?'

'Don't talk like a fool!' Conroy's eyes were bright with anger. 'Since you don't answer my question, I'll make one guess: you're Clint Dawson's nephew. How right am I?'

Mark thought for a moment and then said: 'Clint Dawson's nephew is the rightful owner of the Double Triangle. When he finds out you've stolen his inheritance, he's going to come here and shoot up the whole damned caboodle of you.' He paused, looking at Conroy with his usual cynical smile. Conroy could not be sure whether he was being played with. As he hesitated the mayor spoke up.

'You mean to tell us you're not Dawson's nephew?'

'I knew Clint Dawson and his nephew equally well,' Mark answered slowly. 'Sooner or later he'll be here to claim that ranch and it had better be empty! I'm pretty fast on the draw myself, but compared to him I'm dead asleep.'

Conroy exchanged baffled glances with his men. Then the sheriff asked:

'Why doesn't he come himself if he's so tough? Why

send you to do his dirty work?'

'Too busy, I reckon. Got big interests in the city.' Mark wondered how much longer he could sustain his bluff as Conroy and his men murmured amongst themselves. He was simply playing for time – time to reach his .45s, thrust loosely in the belt of Smoke standing nearby.

'This mug's lying!' Smoke decided abruptly, spitting with venom. 'Let me go to work on him, boss! I'll soon get the truth out of him!'

'Good idea,' Conroy responded calmly. 'Go ahead, Smoke.'

Mark tensed himself as the shaven-headed Smoke swaggered to a position in front of him, the better to get in a series of violent blows. Abruptly Mark took the only chance he had and slammed his bunched fist straight into the gunman's stomach. It was one hell of a punch and Smoke's wind exploded in a choking gasp as his face purpled. He doubled up, hands to his middle, only to get a second blow straight in the face.

Instantly Mark made a grab at the nearest .45 in Smoke's belt, but quick as he was, he was not quick enough to beat the fully alert Conroy. Mark froze as the barrel of Conroy's gun jabbed solidly at the side of his neck.

'That's enough of the games,' Conroy said briefly. 'And since Smoke seems to be losing his touch these days, I'm taking over myself. *Are* you the nephew? *Start talking*!'

Mark's head sang at the slap he received across the face. It was followed by another, and then another, each one delivered with such vicious force he was nearly knocked from his chair and tears sprang into his eyes. For what seemed an eternity he was reeling back and forth, absorbing blow after blow, only prevented from falling out of the chair by a following impact that straightened him up again.

Goaded beyond endurance, regardless of the conse-
quences, he leapt up and tried to whip an uppercut to
Conroy's chin – but in his weakened state he was a fraction
slow and instead he received one himself that flung him,
dazed and pain-deadened, into a corner of the room.
Conroy strode over to him and delivered a savage kick.

'Tough guy, eh? OK, maybe you'll talk if I start shooting
bits off you! I'll count to ten—'

'Since you aim to kill me anyway, you can go to hell.'

'I'm giving you a last chance;' Conroy retorted.
'. . . Seven, eight, nine . . .'

He raised his gun and Mark shut his eyes – but at the
same instant there was a splintering of glass from nearby
as the window was shattered. Conroy gasped and dropped
his gun as another weapon exploded nearby. Blood
flooded on to his palm. His men swung, then dropped
their weapons before a pair of Colts, levelled straight at
them. Mark turned, rubbing his aching head, and saw the
crouched figure of Harry framed in the broken glass.

Seeing Mark's wondering look, Harry smiled grimly.

'I dropped in here to have a word with you and saw the
back of some heavy framed in the kitchen doorway. On
the stairs I heard clearly what was going on in here – so I
skipped back around to the front and climbed on to the
porch roof to take a gander. Seems I was just in time.' He
flashed a glance to Conroy's men.

'You mugs can throw your hardware on the bed,' Harry
ordered. 'Conroy, you'd better tie up that hand. You've
probably lost enough to lower your blood pressure. I'd
like to watch you bleed to death, but my boss here probably won't think the same. I've always said he's too tender-
hearted.'

'Yeah?' Conroy's pain-filled eyes were narrowed with
thought as he looked from one to the other. Harry gave a
start as he realized he might have said too much.

Catching his look Mark said: 'You're doing fine, feller – and you can get busy on your hand, Conroy.'

The permission was unnecessary since Conroy was already using his kerchief to try and stop the flow from his damaged hand. As his men complied with the implacable Harry by throwing their guns on the bed, Mark got slowly to his feet and moved over to where Harry stood inside the shattered window, his guns at the ready.

'Don't use my name,' he whispered in Harry's ear. 'I'm still Dirk Manning to these mugs.'

Harry nodded, his guns held steady.

'Say, boss,' Smoke exclaimed abruptly, 'this is one of the guys Manning shot in the Swaying Hip!' Instantly all eyes looked more closely at their assailant.

'Smoke's right!' Mayor Johnson exclaimed. 'This proves you're a trickster, Manning! This is one of the supposedly dead guys you dragged out through the batwings.'

Mark had retrieved his .45s and was holding them steadily.

'All right, I know you ain't all fools. I had blanks in my left-hand gun and genuine slugs in my right. Just a little deception, with the assistance of Jud Halloran, the gunsmith.'

'Blanks!' Smoke echoed; then he gave a sneer. 'No real killer ever would put blanks in even one gun. Deep down you're a pantywaist, I reckon.'

'Didn't think that when I gave you a haircut, did you?' Mark said, then added surprisingly: 'Get out of here, the lot of you! You can go through the window.'

'You're surely not letting all these mugs walk out of here?' Harry asked amazedly.

'Shooting them now like clay pigeons would make me a genuine killer, and that I don't aim to be.' Mark glanced coldly at the men. 'When I do decide to deal with you owl-

hooters I'll choose my own time and place and do it properly. Now get out of here – all of you. And, Harry, you
better nip down below and clear that mug away from the
kitchen. He must still be holding up Ma Barrett and her
husband, waiting further orders from Conroy.'

'All right, Mark, and then I—' Harry stopped, fit to bite
his tongue out. The name had just slipped out from sheer
force of habit. Immediately Conroy glanced up with
narrowed eyes from studying his blood-soaked hand.

'Mark, huh?' he smiled. 'I reckon that's the one thing I
wanted to know. Mark Dawson is Clint Dawson's nephew. I
know that much from the will.'

'All right, so I'm Mark Dawson and my cover's blown. I
was clapped in jail for a crime I didn't commit. By the time
Harry here proved it and got me out, you'd become
entrenched here before I could challenge you. But I'll
uproot you, even if I kill myself doing it. Now get out!'

Quickly, thankful to escape, the men clambered
through the now opened and shattered window and slid
down the sloping porch roof to the street below. Conroy
was last, and he paused for a moment before attempting
the descent with his uninjured hand.

'There's only one law in this town, Dawson, and that's
mine – and my law says that the Double Triangle ranch
stays just as it is, including the same people in it. That
means Tracey Lee as well.'

Mark's eyes narrowed a little. 'Her name doesn't sound
too well coming from you, Conroy. What does she mean to
you?'

'I figure on marrying her.' Conroy smiled cynically.
'Why else do you think I put Haslam in that place? Right
now she may not be willing, but men like me know ways of
making a woman do as she's told.'

With that Conroy moved on through the broken
window, slid down the roof, and finished up in the street.

66

Mark stood looking down on the little group as it broke up, then he turned back into the room as Harry returned.

'I cleared that owl-hooter out too,' he said, tossing the man's guns on the bed. 'What do we do with all this hardware?'

'I'll get a bag for it from Ma Barrett,' Mark answered absently, and Harry gave him a curious glance.

'What's wrong? I'd have thought you'd be feeling mighty pleased after your narrow escape!'

'In that respect I am – and many thanks, Harry, for the timely intervention. But whilst you were downstairs I learned something. That skunk Conroy has designs on Tracey Lee! When I set eyes on Tracey I made up my mind she belongs to me – or will before long.'

'Yeah – sure thing,' Harry agreed, then he gave a start. 'Which reminds me! I actually came here to report about her, like you told me – and mighty lucky I did! If you want to get her alone you can do it first thing tomorrow morning. She'll be coming into town for some provisions.'

'How the heck did you manage to discover that?'

'I'd slipped into the yard of the spread and was snooping around after dark. I heard what I took to be her stepfather through an open window – giving the girl orders. He sounded about the nastiest piece of work I ever struck and his language made even me blush! The girl was reluctant, but finally agreed to do as he asked under his threats. So, keep a watch on the Double Triangle in the morning and you ought to get the chance you're looking for.'

'Good work, Harry. Guess I'd better ride back to the hideout with you tonight. I'm not safe here any more, and I've put the Barretts in danger too. I'll pay her up – including window damage – and then we can be on our way. Start collecting the guns whilst I see her and get a bag. We may need those guns if things come to a shooting war!'

5

ASSAULT - AND BATTERY

After a night at the mountain hideout, during which time nothing untoward occurred, Mark was on the move again following an early breakfast. He rode hard to a point within seeing distance of the Double Triangle, and here dismounted to watch and wait.

Eventually he was rewarded by the distant sight of a buckboard driven by the girl leaving the spread, and kicking up a cloud of dust along trail that led straight to Macey's Folly. Mark looked about him quickly, remembering that at one point the trail passed through woodland – an ideal place to intercept her.

He raced his horse across the pastures well out of sight of the buckboard. At length he reached the wood, and dismounted. He tied his horse to a tree and relaxed in the shadiness beside a gurgling freshet to await the girl.

As the sound of the horses and buckboard wheels reached him, he stood up, and waited. The buckboard came rattling along the trail amidst the trees, the girl on the driving-seat, dressed in riding-pants and a flannel shirt. A coloured bandeau held her dark hair from before her eyes. At the sudden appearance of Mark she jammed on the clumsy brake-handle. The buckboard slithered to a halt.

'Howdy, Miss Lee,' Mark murmured, touching his Stetson. 'Or is it Tracey?'

'What do you mean by springing out on me like this?' The girl's grey-brown eyes studied him intently.

'I didn't exactly spring out,' Mark smiled. 'I just need a few words with you . . . I got advance warning that you were heading for town this morning, so here I am.'

'Advance warning?' The girl was clearly puzzled, but her mood remained intractable. 'You told me I could find you in Macey's Folly. If I do want you I'll do just that. Right now I *don't* want you, so I'd like you to get out of my way, please!'

Mark ignored the girl's remarks and said: 'Ever since your stepfather set about you I've had you under observation. How's the back?'

The girl tightened her lips. 'It's all right now.'

'I'm not sure I believe you,' Mark said quietly. 'It was the hell of a lashing while it lasted and before I'm through I aim to give your stepfather the same thing back again, with interest.'

'I'd rather you didn't, Mr Manning. That was the name you gave me, wasn't it?'

'Uh-huh. It's not my real name, though, and you may as well know the truth before your suitor Brett Conroy tells it to you—'

'My *suitor?*' Tracey was looking indignant.

'Yeah. I had a brush with him last night. He told me he intends to marry you, no matter what.'

Tracey frowned, then evidently making up her mind she alighted from the buckboard, Mark helping her. She raised no objection as he motioned to a grassy patch amidst the trees and invited her to settle alongside him.

'Get one thing straight,' she said fiercely. 'Brett Conroy doesn't mean a thing to me. I admit I know him pretty well, but I hate the sight of him. It's my pa – my stepfather, I mean – who is doing all the pushing. I'm not tied up with anybody, much less a skunk like him!'

'Glad to hear it,' Mark said, with a serious smile. 'I was going to tell you my real name . . . It's Mark Dawson.'

'Any relation to *Clint* Dawson?' the girl asked, surprised. 'The man who owned the Double Triangle before Pa took it over?'

'Nephew. How much do you know about the Double Triangle takeover?'

'Nothing, I'm afraid. I had no choice but to follow my pa there, naturally.'

'Mmmm – just as I thought. Well, the Double Triangle is one reason I'm here. I intend to claim it back, by force if need be.'

'I'd advise you not to try,' the girl said seriously. 'You've seen what kind of a man my stepfather is, and he has the support of all the men in the outfit – plus the backing of Brett Conroy and his gunmen.'

'It's my rightful inheritance.'

'But it's not worth killing yourself for, surely?' The girl glanced at Mark anxiously as he remained silent. Then presently he said:

'I stopped you this way to warn you not to go back home. I mean to claim my ranch – the tough way, if needs be. That's no set-up for a nice girl like you to be mixed up in.'

Tracey smiled wryly. 'Nice? From the way I reacted when you stopped the buckboard you must think I'm a pretty unpleasant sort of girl.'

'I can't imagine you ever being that, Tracey. I guess you had your reasons.'

'I was scared,' she said frankly. 'Pa might have been following me, and he's threatened such things for me if I ever talked to you again, my first reaction was to try and brush you off.'

'You needn't worry about him while I'm around. Be frank with me, Tracey. Do you want to go back to the Double Triangle?'

'No, but I'm scared to do anything else. If Pa found out I'd deserted him, he'd find and kill me. He's already beaten the tar out of me for far less. You've seen him when he loses his temper.'

'Listen, I've a hideout in the mountains where you'll be perfectly safe,' Mark said, rising. 'I've friends there. Let me take you there now, to give me a clear field. By the time I've done with your stepfather he won't be a threat to you any more.'

'You're asking me to accept an awful lot,' the girl said as Mark helped her to her feet. 'I know what kind of a beast my pa is – but what kind of a man are you? You told me you were known as the Paleface Killer and would willingly kill again. How can I possibly trust you?'

'That was just part of my act,' Mark said hurriedly. 'To hide my real identity.'

'But how else could you claim the ranch, which you say is rightfully yours?'

'Claiming the ranch is not my only object. I've another even more vital reason for being here. I can't explain fully now, but I intend to run the town and clear all the hoodlums out of it.'

Tracey moved away and to Mark's dismay climbed up to the buckboard's hard seat.

'I'm sorry. I don't like deception. It's the thing I detest most in Brett Conroy and his minions, and now you admit you're doing it as well. I'd hoped you might have been one of those rare creatures – an honest man.'

'I *am* honest!' Mark insisted, looking up at her earnestly. 'But my plan depended on deceiving Conroy as to who I was.'

The girl shrugged. 'To me that isn't a good enough excuse for your mysterious behaviour, your name-changing, and your admission that you're a killer. Mebbe the devil I know at the ranch is better than the one I don't.'

Suddenly the girl flicked the reins over the team's back and the buckboard started forward again. Mark was forced to jump aside, his eyes bright with anger. He hesitated, furious at this unexpected turn of events. Then, gradually, his anger began to cool off as he considered the situation from the girl's viewpoint.

So far he'd done little to inspire confidence. He had given himself a killer's name, and told a story he couldn't prove. 'Damn it to hell!' he swore to himself, 'Just as I thought I had the business all sewn up!'

So long as Tracey insisted on staying at the ranch he could not start any campaign or siege against it. She *had* to be talked round! Thus resolved, he sprang to his horse and began to ride it out of the wood to the open trail once more. . . In the distance he could see Tracey's buckboard speeding along in a cloud of dust within half a mile of Macey's Folly.

He'd waited too long and had no chance of overtaking her – and if he rode into the town itself he would probably come out of it feet first. The only answer seemed to be to wait for her on the fringe of the town, since she'd probably avoid the wood on her return.

So he finally dismounted perhaps fifty yards from the indeterminate end of the town's main street from where he could see the girl's buckboard as it drew to a halt outside the general stores.

Tracey herself was deep in thought as she took down the huge shopping-basket from the buckboard and then turned to enter the general stores. She paused as she beheld Sheriff Lorrimer barring her way, thumbs latched in his gun belts, his hatchet face split by an unpleasant grin.

'Howdy, Tracey,' he greeted, disregarding the formality of touching his hat. 'You're pretty as a picture, I reckon. Just the sort of thing this town needs to liven it up, and—'

'Your job is watching crooks,' Tracey reminded him, 'and in a town like this that ought to keep you fully occupied.' She tried to brush past, but Lorrimer caught her arm and swung her back.

'Not so fast, gal! You might at least have the manners to let me finish. You can't ignore the law like that.'

'*What* law? Let me go I'm in a hurry!'

'There's a town law that buckboards have to be put in a side street if you're stopping long. The main street gets cluttered up with 'em and the mayor and Brett Conroy don't like it.'

'I never heard of that law before – I think you're just trying to be awkward. Find Brett Conroy for me. I'm not taking your word for it.'

'Conroy ain't in town yet – busy at his spread, I guess. And I'm telling you to move that wagon.'

Tracey hesitated, her expression obstinate. The thin-faced sheriff gave a crooked smile as he surveyed her. 'Mebbe I can forget the law – for a consideration! I can't see that it's anything you can object to—'

'Get to the point, can't you?'

'Well, I reckon a little kiss would settle it. Been a long time since a gal as young and purty as you gave me a kiss.'

'I'm not surprised, and it'll be a lot longer, too, far as I'm concerned! You're nothing but a disgrace to the community, and—'

Tracey's angry words were cut off as the sheriff suddenly

seized her in his sinewy arms, crushing her hard against him and knocking the shopping-basket out of her grip. Tracey struggled savagely, but she could not avoid being kissed – not once but several times. Immediately men began to gather round to watch, most of them grinning at each other. The less dissolute men who might have done something to stop it were in the background, held away by Conroy's own strong-arm boys who saw no reason why Sheriff Lorrimer should not have his fun. Any sense of gallantry had long since died in the roughnecks who obeyed Conroy.

Breathless, fighting unavailingly, Tracey tried to drag free. A woman hurled a melon as her only weapon and it split soggily over the sheriff's head – but it did not deter him. He merely glared round once, then seized Tracey in a tighter hold than ever.

'Filthy animal!' Tracey screamed, lashing out with her nails. 'You ornery pig!' She kicked fiercely, her half-boot cracking against Lorrimer's shin. All he did was relax for a moment, then he swung her back to him.

'Get him off her, yuh durned yeller-bellies!' roared the old woman who'd thrown the melon. 'The sheriff's gone loco!' The men in the background tried to surge forward to intervene, but could not get past the barrier of grinning gunhawks.

Then there came a sudden thunder of hoofs, causing the men and women to scatter wildly as a horse came plunging into their midst. Mark leapt from the saddle before the horse had dragged to a halt. In three strides he had reached the sheriff, seized him by the collar and dragged him backwards. Lorrimer spun round to deal with his assailant, only for an iron fist to strike him straight in the face. Sparks exploded behind his eyes and he felt blood suddenly stream from his nostrils.

Pushing Tracey to one side, Mark moved forward, his

face merciless. His left shot out, then his right, sending the sheriff spinning helplessly backwards. Before he could retaliate a haymaker to the chin flung him with agonizing force against the buckboard's rear off-wheel, dislodging his hat.

Mark seized his exposed hair, then began to batter his head with murderous violence against the wheel. Lorrimer screamed and shouted, pain lancing through his head at the repeated violent concussions. His senses blackening, he dropped to the dust, blood trickling from his nose and also streaming from his split skull.

White-faced and relentless, Mark heaved up the slack body in his powerful hands and flung it from him. It landed like a wet sack in a pile of manure defiling the centre of the street. Lorrimer, not quite out, squirmed for a second or two and then relaxed helplessly, quivering.

'Better shovel him up with rest of the dung,' Mark said curtly, glancing at the onlookers. 'And if any of you had any decent feelings you'd have done what I've just done. Yellow no-goods, the lot of you. You OK, Tracey?'

'Yes.' She was pale and her voice was nearly a whisper. 'I – look behind you!' she finished abruptly.

Mark swung to find Brett Conroy standing behind him, a gun levelled in his left hand, his right hand heavily bandaged.

'Lorrimer got it wrong when he thought I hadn't yet come into town,' he said. 'I saw what went on. If you hadn't acted, Dawson, I would have.'

'Very chivalrous of you.'

'I'd have done it because Tracey's my girl, not Lorrimer's. But you've made a bad mistake attacking the law: it's a punishable offence.'

'What on earth are you talking about, Brett?' Tracey cried in amazement. 'The law had nothing to do with it. That dirty skunk of a sheriff attacked me, and—'

'This doesn't concern you, Tracey!' Conroy snapped. 'Mebbe you thought you were being gallant, Dawson. But the fact remains you attacked the representative of the law and beat the senses out of him. Lorrimer will know what the official sentence is for that when he wakes up. Meantime you can cool off in the jail.'

There were angry murmurs from the crowd.

'What are you tryin' to pull, Conroy? This guy saved Tracey from that gorilla!'

'We'd have done the same ourselves if your blasted gunmen hadn't been in the way.'

Conroy gave a sharp glance at his owl-hooters, and it was the signal for them to spring guns into their hands. The protests gradually died away. Then Tracey pushed forward and faced Conroy directly.

'You actually mean you're low enough to throw Mark Dawson in the cooler for *saving me?*'

'Nope – for attacking the law, which is a very different thing. I'll look after you from here on, Tracey.'

'I'm not sure I don't prefer the sheriff, or else a basket of snakes.'

Conroy glanced about him and finally towards Smoke Milligan, his bristly scalp hidden by his sombrero.

'Smoke, you can scrape the sheriff out of that muck and clean him up. You other boys dump this guy Dawson in the jail. We'll decide later what to do with him.'

Mark was seized and bundled along the street, into the sheriff's office, and finally into the jail at the rear. Tracey watched the farce from where she was standing, then glanced at Lorrimer as he was indelicately hauled to his feet. A couple of buckets of water did a good deal to revive him. With the water went the horse droppings clinging to his face and hands. Conroy wrinkled his nose and turned to the girl.

'You need somebody to look after you, Tracey, and in a

town like this the safest way is to marry the guy who runs it. Nobody would dare get fresh with the wife of the boss.'

'These hoodlums would get fresh with anything in skirts,' Tracey retorted. 'And I'm not marrying you on any account. To me you're just plain poison.'

'You've only seen me in my tougher moments. When you get to know me properly I'm as sentimental as any man.'

'You're a *slug*, Conroy! Only the slime is missing! Anyway, Mark Dawson told me he's planning to take over this town, so that leaves me a second choice of boss, doesn't it?' She picked up her fallen basket, and with a toss of her head passed into the general stores.

Conroy grinned sourly to himself, then jerked his head to his men. They followed him to the Swaying Hip, Smoke in the rear and half-supporting the still bleeding, groaning Lorrimer.

'Things,' Conroy said, when all his men were in the office and the sheriff lay half-conscious in a chair by the wall, 'have gone far enough! This guy Dawson has got to be rubbed out.'

'Why don't yuh let me put a slug through him and be done with it?' Smoke growled.

'You saw how the townspeople were on the verge of turning nasty out there – if I'd shot Dawson out of hand, we might have lost our grip on them. There's more of them than there is of us if they really choose to shoot it out with us.'

'Then what's the answer? Ain't you got a plan?' asked Elias Marlin. He, along with the mayor, had seen everything that had happened and had come along with the boys to discover what came next. Conroy smiled wolfishly.

'Is there any reason why the sheriff's office, which would involve the jail, should not catch fire? Plenty of buildings do go up in flames at this time of year, when the sun's liable to do most anything in this region. I guess one more wouldn't be unusual. That way the people couldn't blame us.'

'Now why didn't I think of that?' Marlin muttered appreciatively.

'The fire needs to start tonight – when we won't be seen – and before Dawson is sentenced.' Conroy said. 'Amazing how possible the thing is, isn't it?'

The men glanced at each other and grinned.

'Only one provision,' Smoke said, his voice ugly. 'I wanna be the one who sets the joint flaming!'

'Why not?' Conroy shrugged, adding drily, 'I guess you can prove the truth of the old saying – "where there's Smoke there's fire"!'

6

FRYING TONIGHT

When Tracey emerged from the general stores she looked about her warily, but there was no sign of Conroy or his men. Men and women were going back and forth as usual. Evidently an attack on a pretty woman only rated as an everyday incident in the rough life of the town these days.

So, clutching her basket of provisions to her, Tracey climbed up on to the buckboard, and drove it hurriedly out of the town; but when she was well on the trail she drew to a halt again and sat thinking. Was she to go back to the ranch and endure the viciousness of her stepfather, and abandon Mark Dawson, or was she to break free and try and save Mark as well?

She must try and save Mark! If she did not she would be at the mercy of her stepfather and Brett Conroy, whose odious intentions were now clear. Mark – whether he was lying or not – had at least proved his respect for her.

She turned off the main trail along a beaten track with which she was familiar. It led eventually to the rocky regions flanking the mountain foothills. Here she stopped, resolved on her plan of attack. She had provisions in the basket, and there was little chance of her being seen here if her stepfather started to look for her – as he would eventually.

Meantime, in Macey's Folly the sheriff had recovered and, heavily bandaged round the skull, was back in his office – partly attending to his ordinary duties which guaranteed the passivity of the people, and partly keeping an eye on Mark as he languished in the brick jail at the back of the office. So far he had resisted the temptation to kick his prisoner around in retaliation for his aching head; instead he relished the thought of the fiery death that awaited Mark when night came.

It was late afternoon when he had an unexpected visitor. He was lounging in his swivel-chair half asleep, when some instinct prompted him to open his eyes. He found Tracey Lee standing in front of his desk, regarding him intently.

'Hello, Sheriff.'

Instantly he became awake, wincing at the shafts of pain stabbing in his skull with every movement he made.

'What – what the hell do *you* want?' he demanded, then relaxed somewhat as he noted she was unarmed – as she usually was.

'Just a word with you, Sheriff,' she said, settling into a chair near the desk. 'I came to apologize to you.'

Sheriff Lorrimer stared blankly. Whether it was the shock or the pain in his head, something drew out some long-buried chivalrous instincts.

'I sort of think it might be the other way round, Tracey. You looked so purty in the sunlight this morning, I couldn't help myself. Mebbe I went too far.'

'You did,' Tracey confirmed frankly. 'But I didn't want you to get your head smashed in consequence. I guess everyone has their weak moments. Only human nature, isn't it?'

'Yeah, sure.' Lommer wished his head would stop opening and shutting like a barn door. 'Say, I hope this isn't some sort of gag you've thought up to get Mark Dawson out of jail? If it is you can think again. He's going to pay for what he did to me.'

'I should think he should,' Tracey said blandly. 'He went too far, same as you did. He might have killed you!'

'Yeah – that's why we're charging him with attempted murder! Plenty of witnesses to his crime, I reckon.'

'And when does he stand trial?'

'Tomorrow, mebbe. Sweet juniper, my head is driving me loco!' Lorrimer groaned, and pressed both hands to his brow. 'Reckon a necktie party's too good for that louse!'

Now the sheriff had covered his eyes for a moment Tracey let her gaze dart swiftly around the office, just as she had tried to do on entering – only to find Lorrimer was not entirely asleep. There was only one thing she wanted – the key to the jail door, but she could see no sign of it. Her eyes strayed to the new guns in Latimer's holsters, which had been supplied by Conroy – who had also re-armed the rest of his men after the rooming-house debacle.

Tracey was working at a disadvantage, not having dared risk returning to the ranch for a gun and then departing again. And she knew her stepfather might ride into town at any moment to look for her. If she could perhaps grab one of the guns. . . then the sheriff lowered his hands.

'Mebbe Dawson should have his head busted, same as me.'

'Perhaps some coffee would ease your pain?' Tracey suggested, glancing towards the pot on the oil-stove.

'Yeah – could be. If you're as sorry as you make out, you can make some for me.'

As Tracey got to her feet, full of vague intentions to use the coffee-pot as a weapon, she saw something which kept her motionless for a moment. Lorrimer had returned his hands to his head, lying well back in his chair. His shirt had drawn taut across his chest and in the right-hand pocket was the clear outline of a key.

Immediately Tracey resolved to keep to her original plan and use the heavy coffee-pot as her weapon. She emptied away the cold coffee dregs, testing the weight of the pot in her hand. Lorrimer was still holding his head and muttering.

As she moved towards him, holding the pot aloft, he lowered his hands. Bemused though he was, he was not so dazed that he could not grasp her intentions. Immediately he was on his feet, gritting his teeth against pain in his skull. He snatched at the coffee-pot and flung it into a corner.

'Like all the rest of women, ain't you?' The sheriff breathed venomously. 'Can't be trusted for two seconds together. Mebbe I should put a bullet into you.'

'Why don't you? Attacking helpless women seems to appeal to you.' Tracey's eyes strayed to the guns in Lorrimer's belt.

'Only one reason I don't – because Conroy would probably kill me for plugging his girl friend, and—' At that moment the office door opened.

Tracey turned and gave a start as she recognized her stepfather. Lorrimer glanced up too and Tracey took full advantage. With one quick movement she snatched Lorrimer's nearer gun from the holster and levelled it at his chest.

'You little hell-cat!' he snapped. 'I'll—'

'What in hell you doing, gal?' Haslam came round so

that he faced Tracey. 'I've been waiting all day for those provisions for the ranch – but from the look of the buck-board outside you ain't even tried to leave town!'

'You think I care?' Tracey asked stonily. 'You're not my pa, and I'm not taking orders from you any longer.'

'Put that gun down! You're in plenty of trouble already holdin' up a sheriff, and when I get you back—'

'Shut up and sit down! You too, Sheriff! Hurry it up!'

'You cheap little bitch!' Haslam took a step forward.

'Sit down!' Tracey screamed at him. 'Or so help me I'll put a bullet through you!'

Haslam obeyed slowly, as much out of astonishment as fear. Lorrimer sat down too, glaring sullenly but in too much pain to argue.

Tracey moved forward, snatched her stepfather's gun and pushed it in her pants belt – then she took Lorrimer's remaining weapon and threw it into a corner.

'And I'll take that key, if you don't mind.'

Tracey pulled out the key and then backed towards the jail that lay beyond the half-open rear door of the office. She carefully hooked a foot behind her and began edging open the door. The sheriff and her stepfather watched her fixedly, ready for a split second's chance to pounce.

Fully opening the rear door, she continued slowly moving backwards. Mark was at the bars of the cell door, watching intently, evidently having heard the girl shouting at her stepfather.

He took the key she thrust behind her and had the door unfastened in a matter of seconds.

'Thanks,' he murmured, coming to her side, and taking the gun she handed him from her belt.

Lorrimer and Haslam still watched warily as Mark, now taking the lead, came forward into the office.

'Right, you two – get moving to where I've just come from!'

'Like hell I will!' snapped Lorrimer. 'There's good reason why I shouldn't, and—'

'Shut up and get in!' Mark seized him by the collar and half-kicked him across the office, eventually bundling him into the cell. Stumbling, Lorrimer banged his head against the brick wall. It felt as if it were about to burst. He held on to it, the anguish making him unable to continue his protest for the moment.

'You too,' Mark added, jerking his gun at Haslam, who sullenly complied. 'You can act as a nurse to our battered friend here.'

As the cell door was slammed and locked, Haslam's eyes moved to the girl.

'I'll be out of here soon, Tracey, and when I do I'll see that you'll never walk again after I've finished with you!'

Turning away in contempt, Mark put his arm about the girl's shoulders. 'Come on, we're getting out of here before Conroy or his boys show up.'

They left the office, Mark transferring the key from the inside to the outside of the door. He turned it in the lock and then threw it away.

'Might as well delay things as much as possible,' he explained, glancing up and down the boardwalk. 'Let them stew until we're well clear.'

'Our luck's holding,' Tracey said, looking about her. 'Only a scattering of ordinary folks, and no sign of Conroy's men . . . look, there's my buckboard against the rail – near to my stepfather's horse.'

Mark followed her pointing hand and grinned. 'My cayuse was taken so I'll take your stepfather's horse in return.' He lifted Tracey to the wagon seat and added: 'You drive the buckboard.'

Tracey wasted no time in getting the team on its way, Mark galloping his horse alongside. Only when they were well on their way along the trail and had the mountain range ahead of them did they dare to relax a little.

Mark glanced behind him, puzzled, but thankful that so far there was no sign of pursuit in the hot blaze of the late afternoon sun.

Unknown to the fugitives, fortune had favoured them chiefly because Conroy had called most of his men into his office to explain to them how the forthcoming 'accidental fire' would be dealt with. The meeting had taken place at approximately the same time as Tracey had been in the sheriff's office – hence none of Conroy's supporters had witnessed the comings and goings.

And back in town, the meeting was nearly over in Conroy's office.

'That's settled,' Conroy said, lighting one of his Mexican cheroots with his good hand. 'You boys will be at the back of the buildings, ready with water buckets, to stop the blaze spreading. I don't need to tell you how fast this town will catch alight if you don't get things properly organized.'

'We've got it all doped out,' one of the men answered. 'We'll use a human chain system with buckets from the big water tank at the end of the town and—'

'On no account get those buckets from the general stores,' Conroy interrupted. 'That'd be a dead giveaway. Collect all the buckets – and anything that'll hold water – you can before nightfall from as many different places as you can think of without arousing suspicion. Savvy?'

The men nodded, looking somewhat discomfited.

'The mayor, sheriff, and Elias Marlin already know what's going to happen,' Conroy added. 'The sheriff will leave his office at six o'clock, having spent the afternoon sorting out any important papers we need to keep. The rest can go up in flames, including a lot of incriminating stuff it suits us to lose. He'll lock his office in the usual way and go on home. Marlin and the mayor will also be at home, so there's no risk of 'em being fingered by the townspeople for causing the blaze. Smoke here will light the fire soon as it gets dark tonight.'

'That's the part I like,' Smoke said with unholy relish. 'Even if the flames don't wipe out Dawson completely – him bein' in the brick jailhouse – the heat and smoke sure will! A nice, lingerin' death . . . .'

'How can you be sure the people will think the fire was an accident?' one of the brighter gunhawks asked, thinking. 'One slip on this lot, boss, and we'll hang.'

'There won't be any slips,' Conroy said calmly. 'You know your jobs.' He jerked his head in dismissal, then followed his men from the saloon.

Outside everything was quiet, with no horses or buckboards in sight. He glanced back at his boys.

'Good enough time to start collecting stuff to burn,' he said. 'Come on.'

Conroy was completely unaware of how much the situation had changed in the sheriff's office. In the jail at the back of it Lorrimer was doing his utmost to disregard his splitting head and was pacing desperately back and forth in the narrow space. Haslam watched him in the faint light that was admitted from under the door to the office. His close-set eyes were puzzled.

'What the blue hell you so agitated about? Your office can't be left deserted for long. Somebody will be along soon, and—'

'By God, they'd better!' Lorrimer cried, swinging round. 'If they don't, we're liable to fry!'

'Fry? What the devil are you talking about, man?' Alarm briefly crossed Haslam's features. 'How can we fry in here? 'Bout the coolest place there is with these brick walls, I reckon.'

'I'm not talking about the sun, you fool! Brett Conroy's planning to have my office and this jail burned down when night comes, and Dawson should have fried in it. Instead he's switched places with us!'

'Hell!' Haslam whispered, looking about him desperately. 'Ain't there some way of telling Conroy to lay off?'

'Blast it, man, I've been *trying* to think of something – but there ain't even a window in this darned cell which we might shout through, and these walls are solid brick!'

'No wonder that skunk was anxious to slap us in jail! The bastard knew—'

'Quit belly-achin' can't you?' the sheriff interrupted irritably. 'Dawson knew nothing about it, otherwise he wouldn't have put us in here. He's too much of a lily-white—'

'Then why the hell didn't you *tell him?*' Haslam demanded angrily.

'I *tried*, didn't I? I told him there was a good reason why I shouldn't be locked in this jail, then my head exploded so I couldn't think or speak no more.' Lorrimer looked despairingly at the solid brick walls, then through the barred cell door at the passage outside. He could not see into his office since Mark had shut the door after him.

Haslam looked as if he was about to berate Lorrimer further, then he gave a hoarse shout. 'I got it!' he said, banging his heel on the brick flooring. 'We burrow our way out.' Lorrimer had a look of sour scepticism.

'What with? Our teeth?'

'I ain't tryin' to be funny,' Haslam said, delving into his pockets. 'You've got a jackknife, ain't yuh? Same as we all have. . . .' He found what he was looking for and snapped open the larger blade.

'Well, can but try,' Lorrimer admitted, whipping out

his own knife. 'But from what I remember of this jail when it was built the wall foundations go two feet deep-er'n the floor, so we may only find ourselves in some kind of pit.'

'Even if we do it might be good enough to hide in. Let's get started.'

They went to work immediately, Lorrimer less conscious of his headache in the desperation that had come upon him. He and Haslam settled on their knees, digging their knife-blades into the hard mortar that held the brick floor together. Both of them still had hope that before any tragedy could overtake them somebody would call at the office.

This, in fact, did happen, two men arriving during the late afternoon on routine matters of law concerning cattle. But finding the door locked, they shrugged and went away again, entirely unaware that two sweating, frantic men were trying to burrow their way out of the brick jail at the back.

Nor did Conroy bother to check up. Lorrimer had his orders, and he was confident he would obey them. When the evening came he took up his usual position in the Swaying Hip, keeping himself in public view so none of the townsfolk could accuse him of starting the fire.

Elias Marlin, as arranged, had gone home to entertain two cattle dealers whom he had deliberately invited for the evening so they could attest that he had been innocently occupied all evening. The mayor, too, had staggered his wife by suggesting she should ask in a party of her own friends whom he personally detested.

And as the sun went down and darkness settled Smoke and his satellites emerged from their various hiding-places and gathered at the prearranged spot behind an old stable – not far from the sheriff's office – where they had collected their material and kept it hidden. During the afternoon they had accumulated dry brushwood and shavings, a barrel of rancid fat from the back of the general stores, and three cans of kerosene.

'You sure the sheriff's gone?' Smoke questioned one of the men.

'Yeah. Office door's locked, like you said.'

'Right – let's go!'

They got on the move, keeping well to the rear of the buildings until they came to the massive teak props on which the office – like most buildings in a Western town – was supported. The brick jail was different, having stone foundations.

It was these stone foundations that were, at the moment, making Haslam and Sheriff Lorrimer sweat with fear. The darkness inside the windowless cell was pitchy. They had worked until several bricks in the floor had been removed, leaving hard bare earth beneath – but as Lorrimer had foreseen, it was not much advantage for the foundation walls went even lower.

'You God-damned idiot!' Haslam yelled, out of the dark. 'It's all your fault for not speakin' out when you had the chance—'

'Aw, shut up,' Lorrimer spat.

Haslam's fury and fear suddenly got the better of him. He whipped up the knife with which he had been working and flung himself on Lorrimer, judging his position from his voice. Lorrimer gasped as he felt the blade stab twice into his stomach. He reeled dizzily and fell in the darkness, his hand falling on his own jackknife beside the hole in the floor. Sick with pain and fury, he lashed upwards with it. Haslam gulped and toppled forward, dropping into the hole in the floor and dragging down Lorrimer after him. Both of them lay as they were, half-conscious, wounded and bleeding.

Meanwhile Smoke and his boys were watching the fire

they had started. In a matter of seconds the sun-dry boards of the office were spurting smoke and sparks and a column of flame shot skywards, blasting one outer wall in the process. The inside of the sheriff's office became visible through a roaring curtain of flame, the fire sweeping upwards and outwards, then towards the brick jail at the back.

'Bet that'll make Dawson sweat a bit,' Smoke grinned, watching intently. 'It was worth that haircut to get a revenge as sweet as this.'

The other men glanced at each other uneasily. To them it seemed it might be a cleaner way to shoot a man dead – even in the back if need be – rather than fry him alive. The town's main street became alive as the fire was reported. Men sprang out of nowhere, ready-armed with buckets of water. A human chain was quickly formed, leading from the gigantic water tubs that formed the town's supply. To stop it devouring the sheriff's office was quite impossible, but by soaking the buildings next to it with water the chances of it spreading were minimized.

Most of the populace of the town turned out to fight the blaze. Conroy was present among the firefighters, giving directions. It was whilst these activities were in progress that somebody remembered Mark Dawson had been put in the jail. Immediately a party of men moved forward to where Conroy was controlling the human chain with the fire-buckets.

'What about Dawson, Mr Conroy?' asked a big rancher. 'He was locked in the jail, wasn't he?'

Conroy pretended to look surprised. 'Sweet hell, so he was! I'd forgotten all about him . . . .'

Conroy's eyes met the big rancher's for a moment and in the uncertain light he was not quite sure what he saw there, but it prompted his next remark:

'Quick! We'd better see if we can get at him.'

'Ain't no use trying it now,' another of the townsfolk said, with a grim glance towards the flaming skeleton timbers. 'Reckon that inferno won't be cool enough until morning. You can see the darned jailhouse bricks glowing red-hot even from here.'

'Yeah . . .' Conroy faked concern into his voice. 'Pretty tough on Dawson, even if he was a wrong 'un.'

'I ain't so sure he was anything of the kind,' commented the big rancher. 'Fires don't start around here without good cause. Y'know how mighty careful we have to be during the day – but this fire started *at night*, when there's no sun to cause trouble. It doesn't add up, does it?'

'Possibly Dawson himself started it, trying to get free,' Conroy said.

'He'd have to be pretty loco to do that.'

Conroy hesitated over saying anything more to the suspicious rancher in case he incriminated himself, so he turned away and continued directing operations.

The rancher did not say any more, either, though his looks implied a good deal. With his comrades he continued the job of handing over fire-buckets. Once the blaze had abated, Conroy drifted to the point where he had arranged to meet Elias Marlin, Mayor Johnson, and the sheriff. He frowned as he saw only the first two were present.

'Smoke sure did a good job this time.' The mayor grinned, surveying the crumbling wooden uprights and fountains of sparks.

'Stop talking so damned loud!' Conroy spat at him. 'Big Tony over there's plenty suspicious already and he's enough influence with the folks to take them with him. He's no proof of course, but he can still make trouble. Savvy?'

The mayor and lawyer nodded, then Conroy looked about him irritably.

'Where's Lorrimer?'

'Probably asleep,' Marlin commented drily. 'Following that battering he got on the head, I mean. Pity he missed Dawson's funeral pyre: might have made his head feel a whole heap better.'

'We've done all we need to here, to divert suspicion,' Conroy said. 'Let's get back to the Swaying Hip.'

7

PLUNGE OF DEATH

It was dawn before the ashes of the sheriff's office had cooled sufficiently to permit of investigation. By prearrangement, Conroy, Marlin and the mayor met at the burned-out patch at the end of the row of wooden buildings.

Few if any of the normal townsfolk were astir at this early hour. Smoke and his boys were abroad, though, anxious to discover how thoroughly their work had been done.

'Where's Lornmer?' Conroy demanded in irritation. 'He wasn't at the saloon last night, either.'

'What's the worry?' the mayor asked, shrugging.

'I don't trust him when he's out of sight,' Conroy growled. 'Any more than I trust any of you mugs.'

'I want to see the remains of Dawson,' Smoke put in ghoulishly. 'Mind if I go proddin' in the ashes, boss?'

'I don't want you drawing attention to yourself,' Conroy snapped. 'Stay back and leave that to me.' In his undamaged hand he held out the stout ash walking-stick he had brought with him.

Moving forward to the blackened ruin that had been an

office, Conroy carefully began probing in the debris, then looked angrily towards Smoke as he stood surveying the blackened wall of the jail, its iron-barred door still in position.

'Stop staring at that, you bonehead! We don't want any folk who might be watching to see us showing too much interest in that jail!'

'Something funny here, boss,' Smoke said, ignoring the reprimand. 'I guess Dawson ain't in the cell!'

Conroy suddenly forgot all about appearances, as did the mayor, Marlin, and the rest of the boys. They crowded around the cell door and stared within upon the fire-smoked walls. Nobody was in the cell, but there was a fair-sized hole in the floor.

'Hell!' Conroy muttered. 'Looks like the guy found a way out – chiselled under the wall mebbe. We've got to find out quick before the rest of the people start drifting this way.'

'We've no key for the door lock,' the mayor pointed out.

'That damned Lorrimer has the only key,' Conroy fumed. 'Smoke, get over to his house quick and blast some sense into him.'

'Right, boss.'

While they waited, Conroy and his boys kept an anxious eye on the main street. It could not be long now before the people of the town drifted this way to see the ruins – and maybe ask awkward questions.

When Smoke eventually returned he was looking puzzled and carrying a long, thick crowbar in his hand.

'What the hell you carrying that for?' Conroy questioned. 'Where's Lorrimer?'

'He ain't at home. I had to force my way in, and it looked as if he hadn't been in all night. Anyway, since we don't have a key, I brought this.'

Conroy gave a nod and frowned to himself in some bewilderment. The absence of the sheriff was something he could not fathom – but certainly the last thing he thought of was that Lorrimer had been trapped in the fire.

Smoke went to work with the crowbar, ramming it between the door and the iron framework – but even so his strength was insufficient to force the heavy lock, so his boys lent a hand. They finally succeeded in snapping the welding around the bar hasp and the door swung open.

Smoke was first inside, dropping to his knees and peering into the hole. He looked up blankly as Conroy and the rest of the men quickly joined him.

'Two bodies!' Conroy exclaimed wonderingly. 'How the hell did this happen? They didn't get free, anyways, so one of 'em has to be Dawson . . .'

Between them they hauled the two bodies out of the cavity and dumped them on the floor. In a matter of seconds they knew the terrible truth. Both men were dead and severely burned, but their features were still recognizable.

'No wonder we couldn't find the sheriff,' Smoke whispered, sobered completely for once.

'Lorrimer and Nat Haslam,' Conroy said slowly. 'Just how did *he* get caught in this set-up?' His puzzlement gave way to increasing fury as he got to his feet. His smouldering black eyes bored into Smoke. The gunman had seen that look before, and he began to back away.

'Now wait a minute, boss! How was I to know the sheriff was in here – and Haslam? You told me everythin' would be fixed just right. Remember? I asked yuh!'

'You damned, blasted bungler!' Conroy exploded, whipping out his gun. 'You've fried two of my best men and let the one I wanted killing get away! By God, that's about the limit. . . !'

Conroy fired relentlessly, twice. He was in too much of

a blazing fury to care what he did at that moment. Smoke gasped, twisting in anguish as the lead pumped into him. He crashed on to the blackened floor, twitched once, then became still.

The other men looked at each other in the sulphuric calm that followed. They didn't dare move or speak until Conroy put his gun back in its holster.

'Well, it's done now,' Marlin sighed. He looked about him. 'Lucky nobody seems to be around right now – but that was damned rash of you, Brett! Smoke wasn't to blame and he was a good gunman.'

'He slipped up once too often,' Conroy retorted, his jaw set. 'Forget him. How the hell did this *happen*? That's what I want to know!'

'I think I can guess,' Marlin said, musing. 'Haslam might have came here looking for his daughter when she didn't return to the ranch. We know that she was mauled by Lorrimer, so perhaps she stayed near town and came back to pay the sheriff off for his dirty work. Somehow she must have gotten the upper hand and locked her stepfather and Lorrimer in this cell whilst she released Dawson . . .'

'I'll kill that interfering bitch, and Dawson, once I find 'em!' Conroy's voice was chillingly determined. 'We can't rest easy as long as Dawson's free. We've got to pick up their trail!'

'Easier said than done,' the mayor said grimly. 'By now they'll be miles away.'

Conroy shook his head slowly, his anger cooling. 'No. Dawson wants the Double Triangle, and he also has notions about running this town. He'll be hiding around someplace . . .' He scowled for a moment, then clicked his fingers.

'That bitch was using a buckboard, wasn't she? Wagon wheels shouldn't be hard to track in trail dust. We'll take a look.' Conroy paused as he glanced towards the main street where the early morning activities were commencing.

'You got yourself a job, Marlin,' he said. 'Tell the folks that Dawson not only escaped, but set fire to the jail and burned the sheriff and Nat Haslam to death. Lay it on thick – it'll wipe out any suspicions towards us.' Catching Marlin's scowl he added: 'Don't argue! As a lawyer you can convince folks that black's white.' Then he turned to another of his men.

'Shorty, get two large sacks for these bodies, before anyone gets here. Hide Smoke's body in with one of them, and then get rid of all three. None of them has relatives who'll want to mourn them so just take 'em out in the desert and bury them. Get some boys to help you. The rest of you come with me.'

Within minutes Conroy, together with some eight men and the mayor, were riding out of town, following the dusty road to the north. It was not long before they picked up wagon-wheel tracks – and the definition was sharp enough to indicate a fairly recent trail.

'Ain't many buckboards come this way,' Conroy said, studying the prints, 'so these probably belong to Tracey's wagon. If they branch off then she's headed for the Double Triangle across pasture. And if not, we'll follow and act accordingly.'

Two miles further on the wagon tracks did branch off at a side trail – the one the girl had taken on her first departure from Macey's Folly – but they also went ahead as well. Conroy halted and cuffed up his sombrero. For a while he leaned on the saddle horn and looked about him in perplexity.

'Only one answer to this,' the mayor said. 'She must have went both ways. How the hell do we tell which is the most recent trail?'

Conroy made a snap decision. 'We'll keep following the trail we're on and see where it gets us – we can always retrace.'

'What if the gal's at the spread all this time?' the mayor suggested. 'If she is we're wasting time.'

'Unlikely.' Conroy shook his head. 'She'd anticipate we'd go to the ranch when we discovered the sheriff and her stepfather locked in the cell – she wouldn't know the place was to catch fire. Nope – she'll be with that jigger Dawson some place. Let's go!'

Conroy jolted his horse forward and, amidst clouds of dust, his men followed. For once, the good fortune that had favoured Mark and the girl so far was absent. Conroy had chosen to follow the most recent trail.

As they rode steadily, Conroy began to smile. 'I'm sure we're on the right track: this trail leads into the mountains, and we know from Smoke's earlier bungling that Dawson has a hideout there some place.'

'Yeah,' one of the men agreed. 'Which makes us clay pigeons!'

'We're taking that chance,' Conroy told him curtly. 'I'm gambling that Dawson's the kind of lilywhite who wouldn't shoot a guy in the back.'

He gazed ahead to where the range was probing the sky. The rest was greyness in the foothills – then came the timber line. In spite of his earlier comment he eased his gun into his good hand and kept a sharp look-out as the trail went on. Deeper and deeper into the rocks, further and further into canyons and crevasses, until all signs of pastureland and fields had gone.

Finally they came to a point where the rocky nature of the ground had removed the wagon tracks, and pulled up. They looked about them in frustration for a few moments, then the mayor gave a cry and pointed.

'Look! Over there!'

Not far away, deep in an enormous natural cave, stood the missing buckboard, the shafts on the ground, brakes hard on, and the horses gone.

Conroy rode over to it and contemplated it, then nodded. 'It's the Haslam buckboard all right.' He frowned as he tried to work things out. 'They may have left the buckboard as an encumbrance and ridden out of the state, or put it here for future use. Seems to me we'd better leave our horses here and then start looking for hoofprints – and be ready for anything!'

And as the men dismounted, some 200 feet above them their every move was being observed. Harry was lying flat on a huge boulder, on his turn as look-out whilst Cliff slept and Mark and the girl had a late breakfast.

'Say, boss, take a look,' one of Conroy's men called presently. Conroy dismounted and came over. They had reached a sharp, hard-earth acclivity and in the densely thick, undisturbed dust were hoofprints leading upwards.

'That's more like it,' Conroy said in satisfaction. 'More than one set of prints here apparently, which could account for the two buckboard horses. OK, let's see where they lead. And watch yourselves – we've probably been spotted, but I don't expect to be bushwhacked.'

Harry watched until he saw the men coming up the slope and exploring the rocks, then hurried back to the camp in the heart of the mountains. It lay in the centre of an enormous rocky clearing, backed by a large cave. From the clearing there extended a wide, natural slope cut into the mountain face, and at its extremity it dropped abruptly past a screen of mountain bushes into the gorge 500 feet below, the gorge being a valley leading down from the main trail.

At Harry's hasty arrival, Mark got quickly on his feet, helping the girl up beside him. Cliff, just inside the cave, continued to slumber beneath his blanket.

'They're here – on the way up,' Harry said grimly. 'They must have trailed you.'

'I expected it,' Mark said, drawing his borrowed gun and examining it. 'OK, we're ready to shoot it out if we have to. Get the horses well back in the cave where they won't take fright when the shooting starts, otherwise one of us might get belted over the rimrock edge. Better wake up Cliff and tell him to stand by.'

'How are we fixed for ammunition?' Tracey asked, drawing the sheriff's gun from her belt.

'Pretty good.' Mark glanced back into the cave to where two boxes of cartridges and the appropriated guns were stored. 'Come to think of it, having a showdown right here may save me the trouble of trying to rally the townsfolk together to help me kick your stepfather and his outfit out of the Double Triangle.'

'Wonder if he's with this gang?' Tracey mused. 'I may hate him, but I'm not sure if I could actually pull a trigger on him.' Mark gripped the girl's arm understandingly.

Harry came back from fixing the horses and Tracey turned to him. 'Is my stepfather in with the mob?'

'There ain't any man that looks like you've described him, Tracey. There's Conroy, a bunch of gunmen, and a pot-bellied feller.'

'Sounds like the mayor,' Mark said. 'I'd better take a look for myself. You two get Cliff and go to cover. He should have finished fixing up the cartridges by now.'

Mark moved forward, dodging from rock to rock until he reached a higher level. Edging forward on his face he peered downwards, counted the men, and then he returned to where the others were all concealed behind a tall rock near the cave mouth.

'Conroy, the mayor, and a bunch of strong-arms;' he said. 'Ten of them altogether. But I didn't see the sheriff, or Smoke Milligan, which is mighty queer.'

'Only four of us,' Cliff said. 'Not good odds – I reckon we should blast 'em down the moment they come in sight.'

Mark shook his head. 'Not with my blessing, Cliff. This isn't an ambush: it's a showdown. We should have the advantage up here . . .'

He broke off as Conroy's hat appeared amidst the rocks at the opposite end of the clearing as he looked cautiously about him. Mark rose gradually, his gun cocked – but he was unaware that as he straightened up the large buckle of his belt had caught under a jutting spur of stone in the rock in front of him. Tracey, Cliff and Harry did not notice it either, intently eyeing Conroy and his men as they crept forward.

'Hold it!' Mark shouted suddenly, and put himself in view with gun ready or at least tried to. Instead his belt jerked him back and half-twisted him around.

Instantly Conroy fired. The first shot blew Mark's hat clean into the air and the second one spat dirt an inch from his boots.

'Get 'em up yourself!' Conroy jeered. 'And anybody else you've got with you – unless they want to see you dead! Boys, take a look behind that rock. Looks like we've got the drop on 'em.'

Cursing with fury Mark released his gun and then dragged his belt free from the rock. With his advantage gone he was compelled to move into the open, his hands up, glancing back bitterly at the startled girl and his two friends as he did so.

'But what in hell happened?' Harry asked in amazement, standing up.

'I was pressed hard against the rock and my belt caught somehow.'

One by one Tracey, Harry and then Cliff emerged, their hands raised. Conroy's men closed around them and took away their weapons. Conroy himself grinned and then lounged against a large rock, lighting one of his eternal Mexican cheroots.

'I guess this was easier than I'd reckoned. You're slipping, Dawson!'

'You can thank a stone spur for that,' Mark snapped. 'It caught my belt, otherwise I'd have had you just where I wanted you. I'd figured on roping in the lot of you and driving you back to town for the people to pass judgment. The ordinary folk there will be right behind me.'

'Don't count on it,' Conroy answered lazily, closing one eye as smoke drifted into it. 'By now, I reckon your name stinks!'

'What the devil are you talking about?'

'I'm talking about the late lamented Sheriff Lorrimer whose head you nearly battered to pulp. The folks ain't going to feel so kindly now they know you burned the sheriff and Tracey's stepfather to death. Sort of makes you into a two-cent heel, doesn't it?'

Mark gave a start and the girl looked at him in horror for a moment – then back to Conroy.

'What on earth do you mean?' she demanded.

'Plain enough, wasn't it?' Conroy asked sourly. 'I don't know how you got out of jail, Dawson, but I figure Tracey was behind it. The sheriff's office caught fire last night somehow and this morning we dug out two scorched bodies – Sheriff Lorrimer's and Nat Haslam's.'

Tracey looked away for a moment, her lips tight. While she'd had little respect for her stepfather, his horrible end was a decided shock to her. Mark remained unmoved, but he was obviously thinking hard.

'If that office caught fire, then only one person could be responsible – *you*! Mebbe you aimed to blot *me* out, only things went wrong.'

'Mebbe lots of things.' Conroy straightened up from

beside the rock and came forward. 'Now I come to think of it, the folks back in Macey's Folly might still decide to like you two better'n me if it came to a showdown. They might raise hell if you was found with bullets in you. So you'd better go out in a more – natural way.'

'Natural?' Tracey repeated. 'You never did anything natural in your life!'

'Always a first time,' Conroy sneered. 'I aim to create an accident which anybody would believe because it could happen – 'specially in a region like this . . . Ben, Shorty, take two of the horses out of the cave here and ride 'em down to where we saw that buckboard. Fix them to the buckboard and ride back here.'

As the men moved to obey, Mark gave Conroy a bitter look.

'Just how are you planning to kill us?'

'You'll find out quick enough,' Conroy smiled sadistically. 'Meantime, you can sweat it out!'

Ben and Shorty brought out the two horses required, saddled them, then rode them along the ledge and down the slope to where the buckboard had been left. Mark looked about him, but the situation was hopeless. To his rear was the continuation of the broad ledge, ending in the 500 foot drop into the gorge below, and to the front stood Conroy and his men, every one armed and ready to shoot to kill if attacked.

'There's no way out, Dawson!' Conroy said, seeing the appraisement. 'I've got rid of that bungler Smoke, so there'll be no mistake this time.' He blew a cloud of cheroot smoke in the air.

The tense silence was broken at length by the rumble of the buckboard as it was driven up the slope. Presently it reached the level ground and came to a halt. The two men dismounted and moved to one side as Conroy jerked his head.

'Get in it, all four of you!' Conroy motioned with his gun. 'In the back – not the driver's seat.'

One by one the four obeyed, and waited to see what Conroy would do next. Conroy was deliberately taking his time so as to prolong the suspense. He moved to the front of the wagon, and did something with the reins.

'This is the pay-off,' he said at last, moving back to the side of the wagon. 'You'll notice that this wagon is facing the continuation of this ledge, where it dips down into space? A couple of shots from my gun'll be enough to set these two jittery cayuses bounding like hell along that ledge – and though none of you is bound, I reckon you'll never have time to pull the team up, 'specially since the reins are pulled away to the front out of your reach. Should be fun watching you try, though!'

'You dirty, murdering swine!' Harry yelled, hurling himself forward to the edge of the buckboard.

Conroy grinned. 'Better take it easy, feller, or you may go out before your time. Murder it may be, and perhaps I am a dirty swine, but there's nothing you can do about it.'

'I can still do *this*,' Harry answered, and he slammed up his heavy riding-boot straight into Conroy's face. With a yell of pain Conroy stumbled backwards, blood welling from a deep gash on the side of his jaw. . . .

Retaliation was immediate. The mayor fired twice. Harry reeled helplessly, blood appearing on his forehead and chest; then he crashed against the edge of the buckboard, overbalanced, and dropped motionless in the dust. The horses moved restlessly, but did not bolt.

'Harry!' Mark cried hoarsely. 'By God, one day I'll get you for this!'

Conroy got up slowly, whipping off his kerchief and holding it to his bleeding face.

'Get 'em going!' he snarled. 'Mayor, use your gun again. I've got to fix this damned cut on my face.'

Mayor Johnson promptly fired into the air, this time just above the horses' heads. Frightened out of their wits by the shots so close to them, the already jittery horses immediately got on the move in the only possible direction: straight ahead. Conroy, despite the pain of his injured face, grinned exultantly as he watched the wagon bouncing and jumping dangerously along the ledge.

'I guess that'll teach 'em,' he said. 'Neat touch leaving them unbound, so it'll look like a genuine accident'

'*There they go!*' the mayor cried excitedly.

He was right. The three in the buckboard, standing up and struggling to stop the horses' blind onrush, were tackling a hopeless proposition. They became remote as the wagon rocked and swerved – then it plunged from sight, straight over the rim of the ledge.

There was a long, aching silence and then, from far away, a remote crashing sound as the wagon struck the floor of the gorge – a sheer drop of 500 feet!

8

VENGEANCE FROM THE GRAVE

'I guess that takes care of that,' the mayor said, leathering his gun. 'We'd better take a look just to make sure.'

Conroy was holding his jaw and wincing.

'OK, you do it. Take the boys with you since your eyesight isn't too hot.'

Johnson nodded and, with the boys following him, he approached the ledge and then lay down. Edging forward carefully, his head poking over the abrupt termination of the ledge, he gazed into the 500-foot depth.

At this height – especially for the myopic mayor – it was impossible to distinguish anything much against the uniform grey of rockery below – but there was a drifting haze of dust that told its own story. When eventually it had cleared it left a remote but unmistakable brown splotch on the grey.

'Horses, wagon in bits, and bodies too, I reckon,' the mayor said, then he glanced over his shoulder towards Conroy as he half-crouched on a rock nursing his face.

106

'Hey, Brett, come and look. You'll enjoy this.'

As Conroy came and lay alongside him, the mayor gave him a glance.

'Nicest "accident" we've figured up to now,' he said, and received a bitter look.

'*I've* figured, you mean! I'm the brains around here, Johnson.'

The mayor shrugged and became silent, studying the mountain scrub and bushes projecting out of the cliff face all the way down into the depths. He fancied that for a moment he saw something move, but could not be sure. As the suggestion did not appear again he looked once more at Conroy.

'What about the guy I plugged?' he questioned. 'Do we throw him down here?'

'Nope. We bury him in these foothills some place. Can't have him found with the other bodies because the bullets would be found too. We'll dump him as we return to town. Let's go.'

He scrambled up and led the way back to the horses. Then as he mounted he glanced towards the cave.

'Some cayuses there we can use,' he said. 'Bring 'em along and chuck this body over one of 'em.'

His men did as he ordered, then the procession returned down the slope, eventually reached the trail, and began the journey back to Macey's Folly. It was some time after noon when they arrived – minus the body of Harry, which lay buried in the sand off the trail between the town and the mountains.

'What happens now?' the mayor asked, when the boys had been dismissed and he and Conroy had tied their horses outside the Swaying Hip.

'We tighten our hold on the folks in this town, that's what,' Conroy said, holding his face. 'We need a new sheriff to be sworn in by you, after an election, of course. I

107

reckon the only man for that now is Elias Marlin.'

'Unless,' Johnson frowned, 'the townsfolk aren't ready to play ball.'

'Soon see. I'll have some chow in my office – if I can with this blasted sore face – and then go along and see how Marlin made out explaining away the jail fire. We can judge the mood of the folks from that.'

'I'll join you with the eats,' the mayor said, and followed Conroy into the saloon.

After their meal, both men made their way to Elias Marlin's office. His own lunch comprised milk and a beef sandwich. They were perched ready on a stack of legal documents as Conroy and Johnson entered.

Marlin glanced up as he tugged off steel-rimmed spectacles.

'Did you manage to pick up the trail of Dawson and the girl?'

'We did more than that.' Conroy threw himself in a chair and held on to his face, now covered with wadding.

'Say, what happened to your face?'

'I got kicked,' Conroy retorted, and did not explain any further. 'We've now got a clear run in front of us, Marlin. Dawson, Tracey Lee, and one of the guys helping Dawson all took a 500 foot dive over a cliff. There was another guy, but we took care of him too and buried him off trail as we came back.'

Marlin grinned as he reached for his glass of milk. 'Sounds like a good morning's work,' he admitted.

'How about your end of things? How did the folks take it about the jail fire?'

'Hard to say.' The lawyer knitted his brows. 'I got them together in the main street and told them the tale you'd suggested. Most of them seemed ready to believe that Dawson caused the fire, and trapped Lorrimer and Haslam in it – but Big Tony did what he could to turn them against it.' Conroy's rat-trap mouth set as he recalled the big rancher.

'Him again, huh? What was he doing in town that early? Ain't he got enough work on his spread?'

'I wouldn't know. Mebbe he stayed in town to see what came out of the fire. The guy's getting to be dangerous, Brett. He seemed to know even more than he was letting on, too. The folks listen to what he says, and I had the hell of a time convincing them. Not sure I entirely managed it.'

'We'll take care of Big Tony,' the mayor said, entirely sure of himself after his recent murderous exploits. 'Since, in the main, the folks seem to have swallowed your story that's all that really matters.'

Marlin finished his milk and then gave Conroy an enquiring glance.

'How come you killed Tracey? I thought you were sweet on her, Brett.'

'It became necessary,' Conroy replied flatly. 'This town, and the money that turns in from the taxes and the spreads I own, is worth more than any woman. I can get another woman a lot easier than mastering another town as I have this one.' Conroy got to his feet decisively.

'Time to tighten our hold again,' he said. 'Dawson put plenty of chinks in our armour while he was around, and they need fixing quick. Mayor, put up a notice telling the people they'll be needed to elect a new sheriff tonight. You can soon get the notice printed at the *Macey's Folly Gazette* offices. Make it tonight at 8.30. And I'm going to nominate you for sheriff, Marlin.'

'Yeah?' Marlin reflected. 'I'm no gunman, and I've plenty to do otherwise—'

'You'll do as you're told, Marlin, and there won't be any gun trouble from here on – not with Dawson dead. We've got to have somebody who's on the inside.'

'I can see that, but what happens if the people put up

another candidate? Big Tony, for instance?'

'Let 'em try!' Conroy snapped. 'Get busy with that meeting notice. I'll give the boys the tip-off. And you be with us tonight, Marlin.'

On that note they parted, and once he had spoken to his men, and made arrangements to have a new sheriff's office built and the jail repaired, Conroy retired to his ranch to prepare for the evening and try to make a good job of plastering his face.

He arrived at the Swaying Hip at his usual time. Evidently Mayor Johnson had done as he was told, for far more than the normal number of customers began to gather at an early hour – and there was a considerable quantity of women amongst them too.

By 8.30, the time appointed, the Swaying Hip's main room was full. Big Tony was there, looking grimly suspicious – but Conroy's gunhawks were also there in case he started anything untoward.

Conroy climbed on to one of the larger tables and raised his hands for silence. He got it, the men and women waiting to hear what he had to say.

'Somehow – we don't know how – the feller we knew as Dirk Manning, but whose real name was Mark Dawson, got the better of Sheriff Lorrimer and burned him to death in the jail. With him went Nat Haslam, and that too we'll never know about.'

'Not unless you choose to tell us,' Big Tony commented.

'And what in hell do you mean by that?' Conroy demanded. 'You all know I was in the saloon here when the fire broke out. I'd nothing to do with it and nobody can prove I had.'

'Nope, that's the pity,' Big Tony said. 'But sure as I'm standing here, Conroy, you fixed things – only Dawson was too smart and instead of burning him to death by a supposed accident, you murdered the sheriff and Haslam. There's plenty of folks around here who are more than a mite inclined to agree with me.'

'I was in here all the time until I was told about the fire. Everybody knows that!'

'Sure you were,' Big Tony nodded. 'But you could easily have tipped off one of your boys to do it – most likely Smoke Milligan. Seems more than passin' queer to all of us that we ain't seen him since the fire. Where is he?'

'I'm not responsible for him!' Conroy retorted.

'Don't hand me that,' the rancher said. 'You never let him too far out of your sight in case he might say something awkward. So where is he?'

'Up to something on his own,' Conroy growled. 'I ain't seen him since the fire.'

'There's one good answer.' Big Tony narrowed his eyes. 'Smoke started the fire, and to stop him talkin' you rubbed him out. And I can prove it!'

The men and women looked at him in surprise. But their surprise was nothing to Conroy's. His damaged jaw actually sagged for a moment.

'OK, fellers,' Big Tony called, nodding to a group of men not very far away from him. They promptly left the saloon.

Conroy stood and waited in baffled fury, the townsfolk gazing towards the batwings. Presently they swung back and forth again and the men reappeared, carrying something long and heavy wrapped in old sacking.

Big Tony got up and pulled the top of the sacking to one side. Conroy automatically stepped forward, unable to control his curiosity, and he found himself looking upon the grey, dead face of Smoke Milligan, sand clinging to his scalp and, ironically, covering his baldness.

'I reckon that ought to be proof enough for the folks,' Big Tony said, and jerked his head for the corpse to be taken out. 'There's two .45 slugs in it – and you use a .45, Conroy!'

Conroy was struggling to remain calm. 'So do lots of men around here. You use a .45 yourself, if it comes to that—'

'Every .45 has its own characteristics,' Big Tony went on, implacably. 'Mebbe in the way the hammer strikes, mebbe in the bore of the barrel. One day I'll get a slug from your gun and match it up with the bullets in Smoke, then—'

'The only way you'll get bullets from me is in your own damned lying hide,' Conroy retorted. 'You can't prove how Smoke got himself killed, and we're just wasting time . . .'

But Big Tony was far from finished talking.

'Everything I'm sayin' is for the benefit of these decent folks around me,' he said. 'Once they realize you're just a cheap double-crossing killer they'll kick you and your whole damned brood out of town. Smoke was only a no-account owl-hooter, but the fact that he was killed makes somebody his murderer – and that's *you*, Conroy! I saw everything that went on at the jail, including your shooting of Smoke!'

'Yeah?' Conroy eyes glinted dangerously. 'Mighty smart of you. Where were you to keep an eye on the jail?'

'Near enough to see all I wanted. I stayed the night just outside the town, sleeping under the stars, just to see what happened when daylight came. I saw everything you did, and when one of your boys took those bodies out of town I followed him. After he'd finished I dug out Smoke's body. Only thing I'm sorry for is that I had nobody with me to act as a witness to what I saw. But I reckon the folks can draw their own conclusions.'

Conroy half-hesitated over giving his men the signal to shoot Big Tony down, then he apparently thought better of it, and decided to bluff it out. He looked round on the people, struggling to sound unworried.

'You folks can think as you like,' he said. 'Obviously Big Tony is trying frame me, because we've been enemies ever since we first set eyes on each other. It's up to you how much of his lying you choose to believe. I'm here on this table tonight for only one purpose: to elect a new sheriff. I have one nomination – Elias Marlin. The best man you can possibly choose, and one who has served the town well.'

Nobody said anything, much to Conroy's inner fury. In the earlier days, before Big Tony had got such a hold on the folks, there would have been some dutiful cheering and a meek acceptance of the situation. Now there were only grim looks aimed at Conroy and Marlin himself, seated at a nearby table drinking rye.

'What would we want with that shyster?' somebody demanded. 'He's as crooked as a sidewinder, same as you and the mayor there. The only difference between him and the rest of you crooks is that Marlin does his twisting on paper with a lot of fake signatures, and you do it with a gun. Be mighty interesting to know how many spreads have gone the wrong way because of Marlin's handiwork.'

'Yeah, sure thing,' agreed somebody at the back. 'Only one man for sheriff, Conroy, and that's Big Tony!'

Conroy breathed hard. The very thing Marlin had foreseen had happened – but the surprising thing was that the big rancher shook his head.

'I don't want nominating, folks,' he said quietly. 'I've a big spread to look after, and even being here during today and tonight has lost me plenty of money. I just couldn't be a sheriff and do my own work properly as well.'

Conroy moved quickly.

'Since there's no opposition, that leaves only Marlin for it. We can start getting him seconded and then vote on it.'

'Don't be in such an almighty hurry, Conroy. Mebbe there *is* opposition!'

For a moment Conroy was unable to credit the sound of a familiar voice. For about the first time in his life he was genuinely scared, nearly to the point of believing in ghosts. And with good reason.

The speaker was standing close to the batwings, thumbs latched on his pants belt, his face dirty, his head hatless. His shirt and pants were covered in stains and rents.

'*Dawson!*' the mayor gulped. 'Sweet suffering snakes, it's Dawson!'

'But – but it can't be!' Conroy said incredulously.

'Why can't it?' Mark asked, coming forward slowly. 'Or daren't you say?'

Conroy kept silent, getting control over his nerves once again. To the people in the saloon the return of Mark Dawson was unexpected, but nothing more. They did not know of the business with the wagon – but Conroy, the mayor and the boys did, and they still could not believe what they saw now.

The biggest shock of all seemed to have come to Elias Marlin. He was sitting with his glass of rye half-way to his lips, looking like a living statue and trying to understand Mark's resurrection from certain death.

'Take a look at a prize killer, folks,' Mark said, as he came to the centre of the circle. 'He took my weapons, so I'm relying on you to keep me covered in case he tries to silence me.'

'Keep talking, feller,' Big Tony said, drawing his gun.

'Thanks.' Mark nodded. 'I'd slipped into the back of the saloon and heard what Big Tony here had to say – and he's more than right. Not only has Conroy killed Smoke Milligan, he also murdered Tracey Lee and one of my best friends! He also thought he'd killed me. As for that pot-bellied mayor, he shot my other friend dead only this morning, and these owl-hooters of Conroy's around here can bear me out.'

The gunhawks looked at each other dazedly but remained silent.

'It's a lie!' Johnson shouted angrily. 'I never—'

'Shut up!' Mark's voice cut through his. He pointed accusingly at Conroy as he still stood on the table, uncertain what to do.

'Conroy put Tracey Lee, my friend Cliff and me in a buckboard and turned it loose on a mountain pass,' Mark continued. 'The idea was to run it over the edge and kill the three of us. It almost succeeded. There are two dead horses, a smashed buckboard and a dead girl and man to prove the success of Conroy's plan. He figured he'd worked out what anyone would believe to be the perfect accident, granting they ever came across it. But I didn't die, Conroy, and I'm right here to see that you and your damned bunch of killers get justice.'

'If that's what happened,' Big Tony said, puzzled, 'how did you escape, Dawson? Plunging over a rimrock, you shouldn't have stood a chance!'

'There are bushes and tough mountain scrub all the way down the cliff face. When the buckboard plunged over I used the old trick of leaping upwards. The buckboard dropped away from me and I hit the slope and stuck to it, grabbing a bush. Then I had to slide down to the bottom, going from bush to bush. Tracey and Cliff weren't so lucky. They went down with the wagon – all the way until it hit bottom.' Mark fell silent before adding: 'It took me an hour to reach 'em.'

Mayor Johnson almost forgot himself and spoke, as he suddenly recalled the moving bush he'd briefly glimpsed before dismissing it as nothing. He kept silent, looking thoroughly scared.

'Which is why I'm nominating myself for sheriff,' Mark went on. 'Put the law in my hands and I'll drive this bunch of hoodlums straight out of town and string up those who've committed murder. I owe that much to my friends and poor Tracey Lee.'

Instantly the people began murmuring amongst themselves excitedly, then Conroy quelled them by raising his voice.

'There's no proof for any of this! It's a pack of lies!'

Mark smiled grimly. 'Do you people need proof?'

Big Tony stepped forward. 'If you *can* prove it, feller, that's all we need to finish Conroy. Coming on top of my story it'd be the final nail in his coffin.' He thought for a moment, then:

'How's about showin' us the spot where all this happened, feller?'

'I can do that right now! And bring Conroy, the mayor and all the rest of the lousy bunch along with you.'

Conroy's bitter protests were ignored, as the decent men and women of the town, so long under his sway, were now in a mood ripe for retaliation. Guns were brought out and levelled and before they knew where they were, Conroy and his men were all stripped of their weapons and bundled out of the saloon.

Thereafter it was a small army that went riding towards the foothills. Every man and woman who possessed a horse was in the crowd, following Mark and Big Tony at the head, the townsfolk themselves seeing to it that Conroy and his supporters stood no chance of escaping.

Mark kept to the lower trail road and so finally came to the point where the remains of the buckboard lay smashed into utter ruin on the rocks. It was quite plain enough in the rising moonlight, the tall cliff fronting up to the stars in the rear. To one side lay the smashed, bloodied bodies of the two horses, not yet attacked by the buzzards.

'There it is,' Mark announced, dismounting. 'Any doubt about that, folks?'

The men and women got on the move, examining the horses first – neither of which had a sound limb left in their bodies; and then the ruins of the buckboard.

'No denying that this team and wagon took one hell of a tumble,' one of the townsmen said, turning. 'Looks like yuh were telling the truth, Dawson.'

'Smashed buckboards and dead horses are common enough around this territory,' Conroy said desperately. 'You can't hang a guy for this!'

'I've more proof yet,' Mark said quietly. 'The wagon plunged over the top of the cliff there,' he added, pointing up. 'Afterwards I'll show you just what really happened, and also the tracks. Then you can judge for yourselves.'

'You're just stalling,' Conroy snapped. 'Where are the bodies?' There was a desperate thought forming at the back of his mind that perhaps they'd been carried away by coyotes. 'Nothing you've shown so far can be called proof against me.'

Big Tony gave Mark an enquiring look. 'I hate to say it, feller, but he's right.'

'Follow me.' Mark jerked his head and led the way to a more distant sandy region amidst the rocks where two rough graves had plainly been recently made.

'You wouldn't expect me to leave the bodies lying around for the coyotes or buzzards would you? Nor, if you've any decency or respect for dead, will you try and dig them out again.'

'Since *I* ain't supposed to have any decency, how's about me digging 'em out?' Conroy suggested callously.

'No, you don't,' Big Tony interrupted. 'I'll do it myself. Sorry, feller,' he added, glancing at Mark. 'We've got to have absolute proof.'

Mark shrugged. 'If that's the way it is, go ahead.'

Big Tony moved forward to the nearest grave. He

dropped to his knees and scooped away the top soil quickly – and kept on scooping until he came to something.

'Come over here, folks,' he requested quietly.

Everybody obeyed, including Conroy. When the circle round the rough grave was complete, Big David pulled out lucifers from his pocket and struck one of them. The flickering flame and moonlight were sufficient to reveal the grey, immobile face of Tracey, her eyes closed, her features vignetted by the soil around them.

The light went out. Solemnly Big Tony carefully scooped the soil back into place again and then moved to the second grave, watched in morbid silence. Finally Big Tony got up and returned to where the grim-faced Mark was standing.

'I've seen enough, Dawson,' he said. 'That was your dead friend Cliff I just unearthed – and since Tracey's there too there's nothing more we need to know. Let the dead rest in peace.'

'To hell with this!' Conroy shouted. 'None of this proves I did it!'

'I can do that too,' Mark retorted. 'Come back with me, folks, to the top of the cliff and I'll show you plenty.'

Immediately there was a return to the horses and the trip up the cliff face began by the nearest acclivity – until at length the clearing had been gained amidst the rocks where Mark had formerly established the base camp.

'Take a look around you, folks,' he said, motioning to the dusty ground. 'The moonlight's bright enough to see all you need. If you look carefully you'll find the marks of many horses' feet – and you'll also find where the wagon trail goes right along that rimrock there. You know this territory well enough to realize that nobody in their right senses would ever try and drive a wagon along a narrow ledge like that. You will also find by that spur there the remains of a Mexican cheroot, just as Conroy here spat it out this morning. You've all seen Conroy smoking cheroots. You will also see the prints of his boots. Take his boots off and see if they don't fit the prints by the cheroot.'

'Makes mighty good sense to me,' Big Tony said. He took personal charge of the investigation, with a few of his immediate friends to help him. The rest of the townsfolk kept the fuming Conroy and the frightened mayor at bay with the guns.

Presently the massive rancher came forward once more, a Mexican cheroot stump in his palm in the bright moonlight.

'No doubt about this butt being yours, Conroy,' he said.

'So what? Dawson could have easily gotten one of my cheroots at any time and dumped it here after he'd smoked it—'

'And the boot marks?' Big Tony asked drily. Suddenly lunging downwards he pulled up one of Conroy's feet so that he nearly overbalanced. After a moment of studying the boot-sole the rancher let him go again.

'Those diamond-stud marks from your soles and heels are all over the place, Conroy,' he said curtly. 'You're guilty as hell!'

'It's all a plant . . .' Conroy protested desperately.

'I can settle this,' Mark interrupted, rolling up his sleeves and motioning for the assembled townsfolk to give him room. 'Come here, Johnson.'

The mayor was pushed forward. He stood looking at Conroy apprehensively.

'Get your hands up. I'm giving you a chance to defend yourself, which is more than you gave Harry.'

'But I – I . . .' The mayor made a weak effort at raising his fists, then he gulped and gasped as Mark's iron knuckles smote him straight in the face. He was too heavy to overbalance, so he lurched rather like a bloated toy with a weighted base.

From there on he felt the real weight of Mark's fists as he pounded and pummelled him without mercy, finally hammering him hard against the cliff face near the cave entrance.

'Start talking,' Mark panted, pausing for a moment. 'Out with it, Johnson! You shot Harry yourself and you watched Conroy fix the buckboard, didn't you? *Didn't you?*'

'Don't say anything!' Conroy shouted. 'If you do I'll kill you!' Conroy clenched his fists and tried to move forward, but the crowd checked him.

'If you don't, I will!' Mark snapped, as the mayor's head jerked back and forth in desperate indecision. An upper-cut slammed him helplessly against the cliff wall. He breathed jerkily, his flabby face streaked with blood from a gaping cut over his eyebrow. Then again he reeled side-ways from a blow to the jaw.

'*Wait!*' he gulped, flinging his forearms over his face to protect himself. 'For God's sake don't hit me again, Dawson!'

Mark lowered his fists and waited.

'It's right,' the mayor gasped out, straightening up a little. 'I did shoot that guy Harry because he kicked Conroy in the face . . .'

'You don't love Conroy so much that you'd shoot the man who kicked him,' Mark gritted. 'You did it because at heart you're just a gun-happy killer. Isn't that right? *Isn't it?*'

Swung back and forth, his head pounded against the rock behind him, the mayor yelled for mercy.

'Yes – *yes!*' he gasped 'I – I thought he should die.'

'And the buckboard? Tell us what really happened!'

'The buckboard did as you said. Conroy started it off.'

'*He's lying!*' Conroy protested in fury. 'I was having too much trouble with my face to do anything. He started it off by firing his gun. I had nothing to do with it!'

'What!' the mayor screamed, swinging round. 'You damned double-crosser – you *told* me to fire!'

'That's right, he did,' Mark snapped. 'And you, you big-bellied coyote, were happy to do it!'

'Guess we've heard enough,' Big Tony said in contempt. 'You two can come back to town and stand trial for murder.'

The exhausted mayor was seized and dragged dazedly towards his horse. Conroy, standing beside his own mount, watched him with glittering eyes. Then he quickly clambered to the saddle of his own horse and suddenly dug both his spurs savagely into his horse's sides. The animal reacted exactly as he knew it would. It lashed out its back feet like an unbroken mustang, the wild hoofs hitting the mayor violently on the side of the head as he came past.

The mayor went reeling backwards, screaming wildly as he toppled outwards over the ledge. Instantly there was a rush by the townsfolk to see what happened. Mark and Big Tony, being first at the rim of the ledge, were just in time to see the mayor's flying body strike the rocks below and become still.

'Looks like he's cheated the hangman,' Big Tony said. Beside him, Mark straightened slowly, but before he could speak a commotion of flying hoofs swung him round.

Conroy had taken full advantage of the distraction, and was hurtling his horse at a savage rate down the declivity that led to the main trail. Instantly the men dashed for their own horses or else fired rapidly after the fugitive.

The shots missed. Conroy was moving too fast, and the rocks began to hide him as the distance increased. Then those who had mounted their horses went thundering after him in a cloud of dust.

Mark glanced at Big Tony and shrugged. 'We'll leave it to them to try and catch him. If they don't at least the town's well rid of him.'

'He's a killer, and deserves a hanging!' Big Tony snapped. 'We've lost the mayor and I don't like the notion of losing Conroy as well.'

'He won't escape justice – even if not at our hands. Meanwhile we've plenty to do in other directions.'

A long interval followed, during which the remaining townsfolk kept their eyes and weapons on Conroy's gunmen as they sullenly waited. Then the gunmen began to grin as the riders came back up the moonlit slope, their faces grim with disappointment in the moonlight.

'He gave us the slip in the foothills,' one of them said disgustedly, as he dismounted. 'You can get back to town if you like, and we'll go on looking for him.'

Mark shook his head. 'No use wasting time, fellers. Conroy knows he's finished, and will likely keep riding clear out of the state. Call him lost, and good riddance. We'll get down and bury the mayor's body, then head back to town.'

9

MOUNTAIN CAPTIVE

Half an hour later the mayor had been buried. A self-confessed killer, no ceremony or last rites were accorded him. Mark turned to the group of townsfolk and sour-faced gunmen.

'You folks are witnesses of this burial, and that's all we need. And, Big Tony, I want a word with you alone. You other folks can go back to town and we'll join you later.'

The big rancher nodded, and looked at the assembled men. 'Keep a special eye on this snake Elias Marlin. His is one trial we'll be having, anyway.'

Marlin grinned sourly. 'You'll never prove anything. I haven't been in the legal business all my life to be nabbed by any bright ideas you hayseeds might have.'

'Don't be too sure of that,' Big Tony said, and glanced again at the townsfolk. 'Lock them up somewhere safe and guard them until we decide what to do with 'em.'

The men and women began to get on the move with their captives. Mark watched them out of sight, then he turned to where Big Tony waited, the hint of a smile on his moonlit face.

'I've a confession to make,' Mark said slowly. 'I lied to the townsfolk, but I reckon my lies were justified . . . I twisted my story to suit the circumstances. The fact is – *Tracey Lee is not dead!*'

Silence. Then Big Tony laughed.

'I know she ain't,' he responded.

'But how could you know?' Mark gasped. 'You saw her buried in the sand . . .'

'Sure, and she moved quite a bit when I covered her up again – as any living gal would with sand pouring in her face. I didn't say anything. Since I was already on your side, I waited to see what your game was.'

'I'd arranged for her to play possum if she saw us riding back,' Mark explained quickly. 'We invented that effect to stir up the anger of the townsfolk. She'd jumped in the ready-dug grave and arranged the soil and sand around her just enough for her to breathe. Your disturbing and putting it back again was too much for her, evidently.'

'Yeah – but I gave her air space,' Big Tony said, his voice respectful. 'She's got more than a mite of courage, I reckon!'

'They don't come any better than Tracey. The folks all know her, and the thought of her having been killed by Conroy made the folks turn on him just as I'd hoped.'

'Where's the girl now? Presumably she'd get out of there as soon as she heard us ride off.'

'Naturally! She should be higher up in the mountains.' Mark jerked his head to the heights in the moonlight. 'We arranged she should go to a cave we'd preselected. She needed rest and fresh air after what she'd been through.'

'Sure thing. But what really happened after that buckboard took a dive?'

'It happened just the way I explained, only Tracey jumped with me when I yelled at her to do so – and made it. None of us was bound, remember. We crashed into the cliff face and grabbed one of the tough bushes growing there. I don't think Tracey could have hung on for long, but I managed to grab her to me, and she clung round my neck. Somehow I got us down to the bottom. I guess poor old Cliff was a fraction too late trying to follow us – the buckboard must have tipped into a downward motion, taking him with it. You saw his grave. And that one was genuine.'

'I reckon you took a mighty long chance,' the rancher said, 'and I only hope Tracey's OK.'

'She will be,' Mark said confidently. 'Of course I'll be telling the folks that Tracey's alive, but I didn't want any of those owl-hooters to hear of it in case some of them escaped and carried the news to Conroy. No telling what he might do if he knew that.'

'You're right – but what about Tracey? You surely don't intend to leave her in that cave on her own?'

'Hardly! We're going to get her right now and take her into town. By the time we get there those gunmen, and Marlin, will be locked away. She can spend the night at Ma Barrett's. Tomorrow we'll see what we can do about clearing the Double Triangle of that outfit which has been working for Conroy. I'll hire in some decent men from the town instead.' Mark paused and laughed shortly. 'Here am I acting as if I'm the new sheriff, but the folks haven't even elected me yet!'

'I reckon there isn't much doubt about that.' Big Tony grinned.

They moved off, leaving their horses where they were for the time being. And, had they but known it, Conroy was not so very far away either. Having given his pursuers the slip in the mountain passes he had slowly retraced his way, eventually leaving his horse tethered to a rock spur whilst he continued his journey on foot.

He had only one thought in mind – revenge. If he

could somehow blot out the two men chiefly responsible for his downfall, there might still be ways of recovering his hold on the town, providing he could recontact his gunmen. He had no weapons, but there were dozens of rocks scattered around this mountainous area. By throwing some down from a higher level he might very easily wipe out the men he wanted.

So he moved on in the moonlight, the rocks providing constant cover as he climbed higher, looking for a rimrock giving a view from high above the rock clearing he was seeking.

He went along the narrow ledge, passing a series of natural caves on the way; then he paused as a sound reached him. For a moment he thought it must have been a piece of falling rock, disturbed perhaps by his own passage. Then it came again.

It had seemed to come from somewhere below, probably on the acclivity that led from the lower trail to this rimrock. Slowly, he began to retrace his steps. When he came to the edge of the narrow path he threw himself flat and peered downwards. After a moment or two he smiled wolfishly.

About thirty feet below, quite clear in the bright moonlight, he could distinguish the figures of Mark and Big Tony toiling steadily up the mountain slope from the lower trail. Down there, remote. were the outlines of two horses.

He straightened up and looked around him for large-sized chunks of rock with which to accomplish his purpose. His searching eyes settled on a particularly large round boulder nearby, but possibly not too heavy to be moved since it was on the incline that led to the rimrock edge.

Stealthily he moved to it and gave it an experimental push, but before he could do any more there came a sharp voice from behind him, making him swing round in amazement.

'Get away from that rock!'

Conroy knew it was Tracey's voice even as he turned, and the mystery of how she'd risen from her grave was beyond him. But not being superstitious he stood his ground.

'Get your hands up!' Tracey ordered, and Conroy could dimly see that she was holding something. But was it a revolver? There was no reflection. . . .

Conroy slowly raised his hands, thinking quickly. He decided take a chance and strode forward. Immediately the girl gave ground before him. Convinced now that she was unarmed and pulling a bluff, he kept on advancing, making a leap to grab her as she suddenly turned tail and dropped a V-shaped wedge of stone from her hand.

Conroy gripped her arm savagely.

'How you came back from the dead can wait. Right now you can keep on going. Your boyfriend and Big Tony are on their way up, and it's now too late for me to deal with them. But at least I've got you, and that's going to be worth a lot. Keep on moving! Quick – or by God, I'll strangle you!'

Tracey had no choice. She was bundled and pushed along between two towering rocks, then beyond them to the narrow pass along which Conroy had originally come. To scream for help was also impossible since Conroy took care to keep her mouth smothered with his forearm.

'That's where she ought to be,' Mark told the rancher, as they reached the top of the acclivity. He pointed to the biggest of the caves visible in the moonlight.

Mark called the girl by name, frowning as he received no answer. Perhaps she'd fallen asleep after her ordeal.

But he found the cave empty. By this time Big Tony had caught up with him and Mark looked at him with rising alarm.

'She's not here!'

'Mebbe she got tired of waiting and decided to look for us – and missed us. If we look around we can perhaps pick up her trail.'

'To hell with that,' Mark snapped. 'I have to be sure first that she didn't die in that grave through lack of air. I'm going back there!'

He dashed to the point where the upward path joined the ledge and hurried down it, tripping and stumbling in his haste. Big Tony was left to follow behind.

Mark never let up until he reached the grave, then he jolted down on to his knees and began to scrape the soil and sand away with savage energy. By the time Big Tony arrived Mark was looking at a shallow oblong in which there was no sign of a body.

'She got out of here anyways,' Mark said, rising. 'But where in hell is she?'

'Might start looking for prints,' the rancher suggested, and began to inspect the ground – only to be defeated. Except for the sandy area where the two graves were, the ground was rocky and incapable of taking prints.

'Waste of time looking,' Mark said finally. 'I'll try giving her a call.' He cupped his hands and shouted with all his power. The mountain face caught the echoes and flung them back.

Tracey and Conroy both heard the shout as they moved further into the mountain reaches, on the way to Conroy's horse, but the girl was unable to answer.

'Nothing doing,' Mark said finally. 'Let's get back into town. We might find her on the way there.'

Once they had reached their horses they lost no time in getting back to Macey's Folly. The Swaying Hip was still open at this late hour, and judging from the noise from within it and the horses outside the folks were refreshing themselves 'on the house' after their activities.

As Mark and Big Tony entered, the men and women turned to them from the tables and the bar. Glancing around him Mark saw that all the usual gunmen were missing. 'Got Marlin and the gang locked up?' he asked.

One of the men nodded. 'Sure thing, Dawson. All locked away and guarded in that old barn at the end of the street – they can stew there until we've figured out what to do. Have a free drink! I guess Conroy can't stop us.'

'That's OK for now,' Mark agreed, pouring himself a whiskey, 'but it can't go on. We need to establish law and order. Meantime I've something to tell you all. Big Tony already knows. Tracey Lee is not dead!'

There was dumbfounded silence, then excited murmurs and shouted questions. Big Tony raised his arms to quell the uproar.

'Mark had a mighty good reason for saying what he did. There wasn't any other way to get Conroy in a hobble, and to be sure of winning your support. Only snag now is we can't find Tracey, even though we know she's gotten safely out of that grave of hers. Have any of you folk seen her?'

Silence. Then: 'Not bin around here,' a puncher replied, shrugging. 'Not that we were partic'larly on the lookout for a dead girl! Guess I still don't get the angle.'

Mark gave Big Tony a despairing glance.

'I just don't understand it!'

'There's one possibility,' the rancher said, his voice grim. 'We don't know where Conroy went. Suppose by some chance he came upon Tracey? Mebbe he doubled back on his tracks? That's an old dodge to throw off pursuers.'

'Yeah.' Mark pondered for a moment. 'We'd better get a posse together and start looking for her pronto! If he's got her, she'll be in real danger, and he might try using her as a bargaining weapon against us.'

'Certain formalities to attend to, before we do

anything,' Big Tony said as Mark moved restlessly. Then, turning to the assembly he added:

'I'm proposing Mark Dawson here as our new sheriff. I only want a seconder . . .'

Within minutes the formalities were completed and Mark was elected unanimously. A spare sheriff's star-badge was brought from the office of the deceased mayor, and pinned to Mark's shirt. He smiled gratefully as he looked about him.

'Thanks for the confidence you have in me, folks. I've achieved most of what I set out to do in coming here, but I shan't consider my job is completed until Elias Marlin and the owl-hooters have been brought to trial.'

'Job completed?' Big Tony interrupted, frowning. 'Are you telling us that you were sent here on a special assignment? You a marshal, or something?'

Mark shook his head. 'I've no connection with the law whatsoever. . . .' he hesitated, then: 'I do have a reason for cleaning up this town. I came here with that main objective, besides claiming my Double Triangle spread. Later I'll tell you what that reason is. Meantime, what about a new mayor?' He looked at the big rancher. 'I nominate Big Tony.'

Catching the rancher's doubtful look, he added: 'There ain't as much work attached to it as being sheriff, so you can't make running your own spread your excuse!'

Big Tony reluctantly agreed, and once again there was the formality of a vote being taken, with the same unanimous result. The voting was followed automatically by a round of drinks. Mark was anxious to start the search, so he quickly steered the conversation round to the point he wanted.

'I want you to swear me in as sheriff, Mr Mayor, and then I can select my deputies and fix a posse. Tracey's *got* to be found, and the sooner we start the better.'

130

'And what about the Double Triangle?' somebody asked.

'I'm aware we need to clean that up,' Mark replied, 'but Tracey has to be our first consideration. You two fellers,' he indicated two men in the forefront whom he judged to be reliable, 'I want as my deputies, and I also want enough men to make up two parties – one to go north and other south. We'll go outward as far as the mountains and return here to report. I'll draw you a sketch of the mountains so's you can see where Tracey should have been. . . .'

The search to find Tracey went on all through the night, and was as thorough as it could have been, but when sun-up came the weary riders had nothing to show for their efforts.

'There's only one answer to it,' Big Tony insisted. 'Conroy's managed somehow to kidnap the gal. He may even have killed her.'

'Don't be so damned cheerful,' Mark growled, sinking down wearily in a chair of the still-open saloon. 'I refuse to believe that, because Conroy would be throwing away his trump card. There has to be a trail somewhere that we missed, having only moonlight to see by. When the sun gets fully up we're going to look for it again. We'll take a look at the Double Triangle by day, too. Tracey might even be there.'

'If she is, and a hostage, we can't possibly fight if the girl's life is the stake – 'specially after what she's been through already.'

Mark did not answer; he was finding it an intolerable task to stay awake. After a while he stirred.

'I'm going to hit the hay at Ma Barrett's for a bit,' he said, dragging himself out of the chair. 'See you when the sun gets up and then we'll get busy.'

*

Several miles away, Conroy was also fighting sleep, but not daring to doze for a single instant. He was well back on a high ledge, his horse not far away. Tracey lay half-asleep – kept close beside him so he could grab her if she tried to make a break. But although worn out herself, she was only simulating sleep. Through her eyelashes she was constantly watching her chance, her one advantage being that Conroy had no gun.

Eventually, deciding that for the moment there was nothing she could do, she genuinely let herself fall asleep, in order to restore her strength.

She awoke again to the glare and heat of the sun to find Conroy, heavy-eyed but still watchful, struggling to his feet.

'Time to move,' he said roughly, dragging her up.

'Where to?' Tracey snatched her arm free and glared up into Conroy's swarthy, harassed features.

'You're going back to the Double Triangle. Mebbe I made a hasty move trying to wipe you out. You'll make a useful ranch wife there, knowing the place as you do. Since fate has given you back to me, so I may as well cash in on it. Only a fool throws away an asset, and you could sure be that to me. . . .'

'You expect me to become your *wife*! Are you crazy? You deliberately tried to murder me in that buckboard! Do you take me for a fool?'

'I guess mebbe I lost my head there,' he admitted. 'At the time I could hardly try and blot out Dawson without blotting you out too. It's worked out for the best that you weren't killed in that buckboard. I mean it, Tracey. We can still make it as a team.'

'I'll see you in hell first,' Tracey said venomously. 'In any case, Mark will soon catch up with you, once he knows I'm back at the spread.'

Conroy grinned cynically. 'He doesn't worry me. He'll have to dance to my tune because you're a guarantee of his good behaviour. Any nasty work from him and out you go like a light. Now let's get moving.'

'Without breakfast? I haven't the strength after what I've been through.'

'Then it's time you had,' Conroy said sourly. 'You've spent the whole night sleeping. Incidentally, you never did tell me how you survived the fall over that cliff.'

'You were smart enough to think up how to try and murder me, so you can figure that out for yourself!' Tracey snapped. 'And I'm going to have a meal before I go anywhere!'

'Meal?' Conroy looked mystified. 'Where? Only meal you'll get will be when we get back to the Double Triangle.'

'There's the base camp at the lower level where Mark and the boys were hiding out when you caught up on them. Should be provisions left we can use.'

'Yeah – I'd forgotten that.' Conroy hesitated, wondering if some kind of trap were being devised, then he saw the girl was ignoring him and striding away on her own.

'Take it easy!' He grabbed her arm again fiercely. 'I need to be sure you're not up to something—'

'I'm not up to anything! I'm just hungry – and thirsty too! Surely you could use a meal too?'

'All right, but I'm watching your every step.'

Conroy remained alert all the time the journey down to the lower level continued – and finally he and the girl arrived at the rock clearing to find the base camp just as it had been left.

'I'll make some coffee,' Tracey said, 'and there should be canned beans and bread. And you needn't worry I'll try to escape. How can I?'

'I ain't taking my eyes off you just the same,' Conroy commented, squatting down on a nearby rock where he could watch the girl going in and out of the cave.

Tracey lit the oil-stove and tipped the beans into the cooking-pan; then she looked above her at the cliff face to where a stream ran swiftly past.

'Have I permission to get some water for coffee? Or are you going to chew it dry?'

'All right, do whatever you have to do. Nice to watch you doing all the work. You'll make a useful wife at the ranch.'

The girl turned away from him in contempt, a water can in her hand, and scaled the few rocks that separated her from the stream. Still fighting the desire to go to sleep, Conroy watched her slim back as she stooped to the stream – but what he did not see was her swift gathering of a couple of bunches of white flowers, yanking them out from where they thickly carpeted the ground near the stream. Swiftly she crushed them in her hands, jammed the squashed plants, foliage and all, into her water can.

Can in hand, Tracey returned to the oil-stove and went about her preparations for the breakfast. At length she jerked her head and motioned with her arm.

'Come and get it! I certainly don't intend to bring it to you!'

Conroy squatted on a rock as the girl handed him a tin plate full of beans and a hunk of bread. Then she poured out coffee for both of them into metal cups.

'The coffee won't taste too good,' she apologized. 'I missed seeing that the dregs of the last lot of coffee were still in the can. It's a hot drink anyhow, and better than plain cold water.'

Conroy took a long drink of the coffee she gave him, and then made a wry face.

'Sorry,' Tracey said, putting her own empty cup down and hoping the filth she had tossed over her further shoulder would not be too visible as a damp sprinkling in the dust.

'That tasted like sewage water! Mebbe these will help me get the taste of it out of my mouth,' Conroy grumbled, tackling the beans.

Tracey merely shrugged and ate her own beans, watching Conroy as he did likewise. After a while he winced a little, yawned, and then shook himself.

'Sooner I get to the Double Triangle, the better,' he said, putting his plate on one side. 'I'm getting too sleepy to see straight.'

'You won't reach the spread before you do fall asleep, Brett,' Tracey said coldly. 'I've seen to that.'

'You've *what?*' He looked at her dully.

'You've just drunk a nice mixture of coffee and hemlock plants!' she explained, smiling grimly.

Conroy sat looking at her blearily. 'I don't get it. . . .'

'I mean I boiled the plants and used the water in your coffee! Coffee counteracts the full effect, so you won't die – but you *will* sleep.'

'Hemlock!' Conroy gasped, struggling to his feet. 'Hemlock!'

'Uh-huh. Hemlock. I noticed the white flowers growing when I was last here. Now try and follow me, if you can!'

Tracey got to her feet and began running back up the slope from which she and Conroy had originally come. Immediately he staggered to his feet to give chase.

'Come back!' he yelled in fury. 'You can't get away with it, you bitch!'

Conroy managed to cover only half a dozen yards before he reeled dizzily, holding his head, striving to keep awake.

'Damn!' Conroy whispered, as the ground came up to meet him. 'Damn!'

At sun-up Mark Dawson was also astir. He wasted no time shaving, getting breakfast, and then going out into the main street to gather as many of the townsfolk as he could. Within an hour most of them had assembled, including Big Tony, who'd ridden over from his neighbouring ranch. Mark began addressing the townsfolk from the higher vantage point of the boardwalk.

'The first thing is to go to the Double Triangle. And we'd better go in strength, prepared for trouble. Conroy's men will still be loyal to him, but if we move quickly we can catch them before they learn what's happened to their boss.'

'What about Tracey?' Big Tony asked.

'If Tracey's at the spread she'll be used as a bargaining weapon. But if she isn't, then we set about blasting the men who are running the outfit. Once we've taken the place over, we make Elias Marlin write a signed confession as to what happened to my uncle's original will, and that confession will be dispatched to Jefferson City authorities. That will prove I'm the rightful owner.'

'Sounds OK,' Big Tony acknowledged. 'What about Marlin and the hoodlums meantime? Do we leave 'em where they are?'

'Why not? They're under guard and are being fed. Now, those of you who are prepared to tackle the Double Triangle, stand forward.'

Most of the men, including Big Tony, stepped forward. Those who didn't were tradesmen with daily responsibility to the community.

Fifteen minutes later nearly a score of men hit the trail out of town and galloped furiously through the morning sunlight, leaving behind them a cloud of dust. At length the Double Triangle came in sight. From the safety of a grove of trees Mark surveyed it, his men gathered around him.

'Work seems to be going on normally,' Mark said. 'The men are turning the cattle out to pasture, and others are working in the barns and outhouses.'

'Any of you men afraid of shooting it out?' Mark questioned. The horsemen shook their heads, their faces grim. No one wanted to be thought yellow.

'We'll take the place by storm,' Mark said. 'Ride right into 'em and let 'em have it. Hold your fire until we're well inside – we don't want to give more warning than we have to.'

Mark settled himself more firmly in his saddle, removed his right-hand gun from its holster, then nodded to his comrades. Immediately, in one almost solid line, they started the onrush down to the Double Triangle.

Catching the thunder of hoofs the ranch hands stared in amazement for a moment. Recovering from their surprise, they ran for cover, and as they did so their guns came out. Instantly Mark began firing, and so the rest of the boys with him went into action as well.

A crossfire of bullets began to whang to and from the ranch, the outhouses, the barns, and every conceivable sheltering spot. Mark and Big Tony rode straight into the big yard, leapt from their horses, and ducked behind one of the buckboards.

'Pretty good vantage point here,' Mark said quickly, looking about him. Suddenly he raised his gun and sighted it as an unwary cowpoke broke cover. He fired and the man dropped in his tracks. 'Don't pull your punches, Tony. Let 'em have it!'

Big Tony crept away a short distance, peering through the spokes of a nearby cart as he glimpsed a puncher taking aim. Instantly Tony fired and with a scream the man plunged on to his face, his gun flung out of his hand.

'Nice work,' Mark said, then ducked as a shot blasted into the woodwork close beside him. Immediately he retaliated, and thereafter the real sniping began.

Some of the townsfolk had not come into the yard; now they rode in from the back, putting the hastily concealed men of the ranch outfit in an impossible position. They were fired at from both sides and after they had lost several of their number, Mark sensed that they might have had enough.

'Come out and keep your hands up,' he shouted, as there came a lull in the shooting. 'And make it quick! One false move from any of you and I'll shoot to kill on my authority as sheriff of Macey's Folly.'

As he glanced about him he caught sight of a half-dozen or so of the outfit, who had been at work on the further fringe of the corrals, making good their escape across pasture as fast as they could go. Big Tony also saw them and gave Mark a questioning look.

'Let 'em go just as long as they're away from here. We need all our boys to keep this mob subdued.'

By degrees, from their various holes and corners, men emerged with their hands raised. They were promptly relieved of their guns as Mark came from cover and advanced towards them.

'Who's the foreman here?' he snapped. A thick-necked man with a beefy red face gave him a bitter look.

'OK, feller – where's Tracey Lee?'

The man looked surprised. 'Am I supposed ter know? None of us have seen her for a couple days – nor our boss, Mr Haslam, either.'

'You'll never see Haslam again – he's dead. And you're no longer working here either because this is my spread.'

'The hell it is!'

'You heard what I said, feller. You and your boys are going into town to be tried by the people, along with Elias Marlin and a bunch of gunhawks. If you don't give us any more trouble, I might allow that you've worked here because you were forced to and not necessarily because you're a bunch of crooks. But you're finished here now. Fellers,' Mark called to his men, 'round 'em up every-

where you can and get 'em back to town – if that barn's big
enough to hold 'em.'

'If not, there's plenty more barns, Sheriff.' One of the
men grinned, and with his comrades he went off to search
for stragglers.

'Watch this bunch while I look for Tracey,' Mark said to
Big Tony. 'This guy may be lying, though if Tracey was
being held here, I'd have expected her to have been
brought out to stop us shooting.'

Gun in hand Nick hurried over to the ranch house and
up the steps. Once inside, he went quickly from room to
room, examining all the concealed spots, including
wardrobes and cupboards – but there was no sign of
Tracey. Despondent, he came outside once more and
joined the gathering in the yard. Big Tony read his expression.

'No dice, Mark? I've already been through the
outhouses and bunkhouse while you were inside. She ain't
there, either.'

'Then we'll just have to look further afield,' Mark said
decisively. 'I'll want half of you men to stay here and run
this place until I can get a proper outfit together. I'll see
you are paid for it. The cattle have to be looked after,
remember.

'The rest of us are going to look for Tracey if we have to
upturn every damned rock in the territory. You, Big Tony,
can come with me – but before we do anything take this
bunch back to town and lock 'em up. While you're doing
that I'll see that these few who got themselves killed have
a civilized burial in the far pasture.'

Meantime, the half-dozen or so men who had escaped the
ranch when the onslaught had been made upon it were
hurrying across the grazing land, using trees as cover to
commence with, then gradually becoming bolder as they

realized they were not being pursued. Eventually they had reached the main trail that connected Macey's Folly with the mountains.

'Well, Buck, what's next?' one of them asked, his face grim. 'We've no cayuses or chow, and it sure ain't safe to return fur any. If you ask me we've come a durned sight further than we needed to.'

'Nobody did ask yuh, so shut up.' Buck, thin and lanky, looked about him. 'Only one thing we c'n do,' he decided, 'and that's ask the boss what happens next. We ain't so far from his spread – the Blazin' C – that we can't reach it on foot.'

Disgruntled at the prospect of having to tramp several miles in the scorching heat they turned and started along the trail. They scarcely spoke to each other as they went, still recovering from the shock they had received when the Double Triangle had been so suddenly attacked.

Presently they became aware of the approach of a galloping horse from somewhere in the rear. Buck stopped and looked behind him.

'Some saddle tramp riding by,' he said. 'We can make use of that horse of his. Into the ditch – quick!'

They scattered into concealment, their guns ready. The sound of the speeding horse came nearer, and nearer still, until the distant speck of the rider and mount became visible through the dust haze.

'Hold it!' Buck ordered, watching keenly. 'Unless I'm crazy, that rider's Tracey Lee! Leave this to me.'

Buck waited until the girl and her horse were nearly level, then he sprang out and fired in the air once to make his meaning unmistakable. Startled, Tracey drew up sharp as the remainder of the gunmen came into view.

'Howdy, Tracey!' Buck said drily. Then his tone hardened with suspicion. 'You're ridin' Mr Conroy's horse – how come?'

140

'Your place is at the ranch, not asking me questions,' Tracey answered curtly, since by now she recognized all the men as being from the Double Triangle outfit. 'What's the idea of the hold-up?'

'We're in need of horseflesh,' Buck answered, studying her. 'Why needn't concern yuh. Get down from that cayuse, Tracey.'

'I'll be damned—'

'*Get down*! I ain't takin' no back answers from a dame!'

Tracey obeyed reluctantly.

'You've bin missing from the spread quite a time, Tracey,' Buck continued. 'So's Mr Haslam – and I reckon Mr Conroy hasn't visited either. Where've they all gone, huh?'

'Brett Conroy knows me well enough to lend me his horse if I need it, doesn't he? And he's at his ranch, far as I know.'

'His ranch? You're comin' from the opposite direction – from the mountains! You're lyin', Tracey! Some mighty queer things goin' on around here – including an attack on the Double Triangle by gunmen. They've taken the spread over.'

'They have?' Tracey's eyes went wider. 'Where did they come from?'

'They came from Macey's Folly, but who they are I was too far off to notice. We got out quick. Say, you and your stepfather never hit it off. Mebbe yuh did something to get even with him?'

Tracey faced Buck angrily, looking rather like an enraged sparrow in front of a vulture.

'How dare you – a paid worker at the ranch – presume to question me?'

'Last time I saw you, Tracey,' Buck said, thinking laboriously, 'you was goin' into town to get provisions. Mr Haslam set off – blazin' mad – to look for you when you didn't return! Now you turn up on Brett Conroy's horse, looking as if you'd been cleaning out a stable and rollin' around in it! *What's goin' on?*'

As Tracey ignored his questions and tried to remount her horse, Buck grabbed her, and dragged her down again. She gave a little gasp as he added a twisting motion to his hold.

'I never had much time fur you, Tracey' he went on viciously. 'Tell me straight where the boss is, or else. . . .' He increased the pressure, forcing the girl to her knees. At last she could stand it no longer.

'Brett's in the foothills! I left him there.'

Buck let go suddenly. Tracey grasped her aching arm and slowly straightened up again, tears of pain still wet on her lashes. Buck studied her fixedly, his brutish mind evolving fresh plans.

'What's the boss doin' in the foothills? Talk, unless you want me to work on your other arm. . . .'

'Hiding, if you must know.' Tracey was no longer in any condition to keep up her defiance. 'Mark Dawson – or maybe you only know him as Dirk Manning – has taken over control in Macey's Folly, and he probably attacked the Double Triangle as well.'

'You mean this Dawson's sheriff now?'

'He is. And he'll sweep this entire territory clean of hoodlums like you. Now get out of my way—'

'You crazy?' Buck asked drily. 'If the boss is in the foothills I want to know exactly where. Mebbe he's in trouble, and needs his horse back. We'll go back there and you'll show us where he is – or else.'

'But you've no horses!' Tracey protested, still trying to evade the issue.

'We've got one here, and you and me'll ride it. The boys can follow on foot.'

The remaining men glanced at one another and

scowled, but they seemed to accept Buck as their leader.
Buck swung to the horse, swept Tracey up in front of him
and then began riding. In a matter of minutes the men
toiling on foot had been left behind.

Tracey was silent, utterly despondent. After coming so
near to making contact with Mark again, and then losing
it, she had as good as lost interest in future events.

Eventually they came to the foothills, and soon the
pastures were left behind and they were in the midst of
rock spurs and twisting upward acclivities.

'Which way now, or do I have to beat it out of you?'
Buck growled.

Tracey pointed above. 'Follow through up there and
see what you get.'

The rock clearing was at last reached; Conroy was still
lying practically in the position in which he had fallen when
the drugging power of the hemlock had caught up on him.

'What's gotten into the boss?' Buck demanded, dropping down from the saddle.

Tracey shrugged. 'For all I know – or care – he may be
dead. By no means impossible since he swallowed some
hemlock.'

Buck twirled around and then dragged the girl down
from the horse. 'I guess you're a nastier little bitch than
I'd figured!' he spat. 'If the boss is dead I'll sure make you
smart! Get moving!'

He made the girl walk in front of him until Conroy had
been reached. He kept his gun ready, his free hand feeling
at Conroy's chest experimentally.

'He ain't dead, anyways,' he said. 'Just as well for you.'

Tracey shrugged and folded her arms, her face expressionless as Buck went to work to try and revive the doped
man, slapping and pinching him. He kept it up for quite a
time until at last he was rewarded and Conroy opened his
eyes.

'What the hell. . . ?' he whispered. 'I feel as though somebody slugged me.'

'Somebody did, boss,' Buck answered, his tone now altered to one of respect. Conroy passed a dry tongue round his lips and peered at Buck in the sunlight. 'I've got Tracey here and she admitted she gave you hemlock,' Buck added. 'Give me the word and I can go to work on her for you.'

'Tracey?' Conroy's head seemed to clear a little. He looked up to where the girl was studying him in silent contempt. Buck gave her a vicious glance.

'If you want me to pay her off for—'

'Shut up a minute, Buck: you talk too much and my head is going like a buzz-saw. Just help me up.' Conroy struggled to his feet, swayed for a moment, and then got a grip on himself.

'I'll do the punishing of her myself,' he said slowly. 'That can come gradually, through the years, whilst she's married to me. As her husband I can make her smart over and over again for what she tried to do to me. And I asked you a question, Buck. What are you doing here?'

Buck immediately explained, Conroy gradually recovering as he did so.

'By now Dawson'll have the full backing of the townsfolk,' Buck finished. 'So what do we do?'

Conroy gave a cynical smile. 'We ain't running away. We're going to stand our ground, Buck. I'm taking over the Double Triangle again, and I'm going to go on living at my own spread, the Blazing C. I'm not walking out on all that!'

'And if this guy Dawson, or whatever his name is, comes a-proddin' for you, what then?'

'He *won't*, not as long as I've got Tracey for insurance. Any attack on me or the property I own will finish her too.

I've got too many interests to leave behind just because this guy Dawson says so – only I had to run for it whilst I'd no bargaining weapon. Now it's different. The first thing we do is retake the Double Triangle. How many men are watching it?'

'No idea. From the way things were lookin' I guess all our boys have been kicked out. But there's seven of 'em got away with me – following me on foot. Guess it'll be some time till they catch up.'

'Seven,' Conroy mused. 'Nine with you and me. . . . What happened to Elias Marlin and the rest of my boys?'

'I've no idea, boss.'

Conroy looked at him in disgust. 'Mighty big help, ain't you? Pity about Marlin and the boys,' he went on irritably. 'They've probably been incarcerated, but we might get 'em free. They'd help swell our numbers. And I need some hardware, and so will they.'

Buck nodded. 'What about getting men from your own ranch?'

'Safer to leave them guarding it in case Dawson tries anything. OK, then,' Conroy continued, 'here's what we do. We'll stick around here where we've got plenty of cover – and some canned food and a stream to drink from – until your men get here. Then we'll head for Macey's Folly tonight under cover of darkness. We'll have to walk it since we've only one horse between us. Since they ain't likely to expect us in town, we might be able to get the rest of the boys free – and make Jud Halloran give us all the hardware we need.'

'Yeah, mebbe we could manage it,' Buck agreed. 'But what about Tracey? She'll try and give us away for sure!'

Conroy grinned. 'Tracey will be with us, Buck, but in no position give us away. With her wrists and ankles bound and a gag in her mouth I reckon she'll keep quiet. What do you think, Tracey?'

145

The girl made no answer. She knew that she had completely lost the initiative.

10

FINAL SKIRMISH

It was mid-afternoon when Mark, at the head of the search party, returned to the Double Triangle. He was in a grim and almost desperate mood, having found no sign of Tracey.

Mark was reasonably sure that Conroy wouldn't dare try anything in Macey's Folly with everybody waiting to pounce on him if he showed up. Having left deputies in town, he decided to stay at the ranch safeguarding his own property and being ready for a chance to save Tracey. He felt it was only a matter of time before Conroy made his move against him.

Big Tony left to attend to his neglected ranch – and to make future arrangements there for when he took up his mayoral duties – with a promise to return to the ranch that evening.

Mark watched the rancher depart, then he stood thinking for a moment. There seemed to be nothing for it but to attend to more personal matters – a meal, for instance. So, with the help of two of the boys, he went to work in the kitchen, and it was here that he ran into trouble of a totally different kind. There were relatively few supplies –

Tracey having not returned with fresh provisions – but between the three of them they finally contrived a meal of sorts.

After their meal the boys departed to attend to the cattle whilst Mark spent some time thinking out his future moves. There was the trial of Elias Marlin and the gunmen with him, then there was the matter of a reward to be put out for the capture of Brett Conroy. His property, too, had to be legally disposed of. There was potential danger too, at the Blazing C, not so very far away and run by the residue of Conroy's men, whom it was impossible legally to dislodge.

At sunset Big Tony returned. He came into the ranch house living-room and tossed down his hat.

'Nothing happened?' he enquired.

'Nothing.' Mark rolled himself a cigarette. 'I'm killing time working out my problems, but I can't get Tracey off my mind. I was thinking I might ride to Jefferson City and get some of the lawmen to help me. They've got resources and communications, which we haven't. Mebbe I should have done that in the first place, only I felt completely sure of my own abilities.'

Big Tony reflected. 'We still don't know where Conroy is hanging out, and if he spotted you hitting the trail I wouldn't give a red cent for your chances. If you get shot in the back that's the finish. Forget it, Mark. We'll just have to wait it out.'

At about this time Conroy was on the move, half-way to Macey's Folly. With him were Buck, the seven men who were, despite a short rest at the mountain camp, by now nearly too footsore to go any further, and Tracey, mounted on the only horse. Not because Conroy had any chivalrous feelings towards her but because it was the surest way to deal with her. With her ankles tied to the stirrups and her wrists fastened behind her there was nothing she could do – and the tight gag rammed between her teeth prevented any chance of her shouting a warning.

It was completely dark by the time the weary party reached the outskirts of Macey's Folly, by then tired men, grumbling bitterly until threats from Conroy quelled their mutterings. Grimly he addressed them:

'The first thing we want to do is get more guns, so we'd better see if we can bust into Halloran's place. Give me your gun, Buck.'

Buck handed it over and Conroy jerked his head. Thereafter his men followed him without passing any comment until they had come to the rear of the buildings flanking one side of the main street.

'That's Halloran's there, with the light in the back window,' Conroy said, nodding towards it. 'We'll surprise the guy before he can raise the alarm. You'd better leave it to me. The rest of you wait here and come when I whistle. When that happens two of you stay to guard the girl.'

With that he glided forward into the darkness and presently gained the yard at the back of the gunsmith's house. He had just dropped on the other side of the gate before it dawned upon him that there was a powerful mastiff to deal with. With a monstrous commotion of barking it pounced on him from a big kennel in a corner of the yard.

Conroy staggered backwards, just evading the snarling jaws as they clicked in front of his throat. He jabbed out with his gun, kicked savagely, and managed to fling the beast a slight distance away from him. By the time it had sprung again he was ready. He fired, regardless of the noise, since the alarm had already been raised.

Whimpering with pain, the dog collapsed. Conroy strode over it and to the back door of the house just as it opened and Halloran looked outside in the reflected light from the kitchen window, a gun in his hand, but pointed downward. That proved his undoing.

'Get back in there, you!' Conroy snapped at him. 'You're covered!'

He had the advantage and took it. He kept his gun levelled, forcing the startled gunsmith back into the little room where his wife, in the midst of sewing, sat gazing in awe. Conroy eyed Halloran and his wife for a moment and then jerked his head.

'Into the store, the pair of you,' he ordered. The six-shooter saw to it that he had his way. Once in the store he used the reflected light from the kitchen to glance about him, saw there was everything he needed, and nodded to himself. Then he moved, took down a lariat from a number of them hanging for sale on a hook, and made a one-handed tie of the gunsmith and his wife, fastening them back to back. This done he slipped his gun in his belt and used a couple of new kerchiefs for gags.

'I don't aim to blast either of you,' he said. 'You're a useful man, Halloran, as a gunsmith – and I don't wipe out useful men. When I take this town over again, I'll have need of you. Meantime you'll stay quiet.'

With that he strode quickly through the kitchen, over the dead dog in the yard, and then pulled open the gate. Putting his fingers in his mouth, he gave the prearranged whistle signal. Buck was the only one who appeared, hurrying out of the darkness.

'Where the hell's the rest of 'em?' Conroy demanded. 'Doesn't take all of them to guard Tracey does it?'

'That's it, boss,' Buzz broke in, panting for breath and gesturing vaguely. 'She ain't here now! It was you firing at the dog as did it! The cayuse took fright and bolted with Tracey fastened to it—'

'To hell with that for a tale!' Conroy broke in furiously. 'Surely you could have held a damned horse in place?'

'It wasn't that easy, boss. The cayuse was a little ways off and it got on the move before we could reach it because the gal jabbed it with her heels – her feet were only bound to the stirrups, remember. The boys knew you wouldn't want to lose the gal, so they went after her and—'

'You infernal bonehead!' Conroy panted. 'Lost the gal, and the boys gone too. If I wasn't so much in need of help I'd put a slug into you like I did Smoke for the same sort of bungling!'

Buck's expression changed, but he did not say anything. Conroy forced calmness upon himself and motioned.

'Come with me. We'll have to work this out by ourselves. Quick!'

'Yeah, but I was. . . .'

Buck was cut short by a sudden cry from the rear of one of the buildings.

'Two guys there!' came a yell. Revolver fire followed instantly, and Conroy dived back into the gunsmith's yard, dragging Buck after him.

'Into the store,' Conroy said briefly. 'My having to shoot that damned dog has alerted them.'

They tumbled into the kitchen, slammed and bolted the door and then hurried through to the store. Conroy moved around agitatedly, shifting the stock around to find what he wanted. Tied as they were, the gunsmith and his wife could not do anything to help the situation for themselves.

'This is what I want,' muttered Conroy, and by the reflected light he spent a few moments selecting three .45s with the necessary bullets. He handed two of the guns to Buck, retained one to add to the one in his hand, and hurried back into the kitchen to put out the oil-lamp.

'OK,' he said, returning to Buck's side. 'We're going to fight it out. It's the only way. Mebbe we can use Halloran and his wife here for hostages.'

Conroy glanced towards them, only visible as dim shadows in the kerosene glow filtering through the sun-rotted blinds at the store windows. Then he swung round as a bullet splintered the glass of the window nearest him.

'This is it,' he muttered, glancing at Buck. 'Find a good position to start firing back.'

Way back at the Double Triangle all was quiet – far too quiet for Mark's liking, keyed up as he was for something to happen.

'I begin to think we're on the wrong horse,' he told Big Tony, as he came out to join him on the porch. 'Conroy could never have a better chance than this. A thick mist tonight, and yet he doesn't take advantage of it. I just don't understand it. . . .'

Mark broke off. The sound of fast-moving hoof beats had come on the still air. In a matter of seconds they became louder as somebody came riding along the trail.

'I'm going to see who that is,' Mark said, moving forward quickly.

'Take care it ain't Conroy!' Big Tony called after him.

Ignoring the warning Mark hurried down the porch steps, swung to his horse and then galloped it out of the big yard. By the time he had reached the trail that ran beyond a small beaten pathway leading to the main Macey's Folly trail from the mountains, the sound of the hoof beats was entirely clear. It was coming from the pastureland itself. Promptly Mark headed in their direction, giving his horse all it had got to keep within hearing of the hoof beats.

Gradually he narrowed the distance, and at length he saw the fleeing rider against the stars. There was something peculiarly erect about the figure, as though it were a dummy fastened to the saddle. For a moment Mark wondered if some kind of decoy had been pulled to deplete the watchers at the Double Triangle – then, as he caught up, he realized the truth.

'Tracey!' he gasped, half in horror and half in relief.

He caught at the panicked horse's reins, dragging hard upon them until he was yanked from his own saddle. He swung and pulled, keeping free of the flying hoofs and at last forcing the animal to a standstill.

Mark pulled out his knife and slashed through the ropes holding Tracey to the saddle. He caught her in his arms as she slid downwards.

'Tracey!' He pulled the gag from her mouth. 'How the hell did you ever get in this mess?'

'Brett Conroy found me in the hills,' Tracey panted. 'He tied me to the horse and went back into the town. . . .' She paused as Mark listened intently, his face grim. 'A revolver shot in town made the horse bolt for it, and it being Brett's horse I think it was heading back in the direction of his ranch. I was pursued for a while, but as the men were on foot the horse soon lost them. . . .' Tracey paused again, breathing hard as Mark held her tightly.

'Conroy was planning to do quite a lot to me, if that horse hadn't bolted. Last I saw of him he was sneaking into Halloran's the gunsmith's. He's gotten some idea about taking the town over again.'

Mark wasted no more time. He hoisted the girl on to his own horse and rode the now quieted animal to which Tracey had been tied. In ten minutes they had returned to the Double Triangle. One of the men came running out of the gloom as Mark lifted Tracey down from the saddle.

'Say, Sheriff, there's some shootin' goin' on in town! Listen! Been like that for the last ten minutes or so.'

Silence for a moment, then they all distinctly heard the sound of the shots carried on the wind in the still night. In the distance, over the trees, the faint glow of the town's streetlights could just be seen.

'Sounds like the shooting war has started at last,' Mark said. 'Get Big Tony – and take Tracey here into the house. She can go to her own room and clean herself up. See she gets a good meal and guard her with your life.'

'No! I'm coming with you!'

'Can't be done, sweetheart.' Mark shook his head resolutely. 'This is the showdown between Conroy and myself I reckon – with one of us finishing up as boss, and the other probably dead. No place for a girl.'

Tracey reluctantly departed with the cowpoke, leaving Mark chafing with impatience until Big Tony suddenly appeared astride his horse.

'We're riding into town, Tony. I've got it straight from Tracey that Conroy's returned, and from the sound of things he's either shooting the place up or else stopping the hell of a lot of lead himself. Let's go!'

'What about taking some of the boys?'

'No. I'm taking no chances on leaving this spread depleted now Tracey's back. Anyway, the townsfolk will be with us in Macey's Folly.'

The two men rode swiftly until the main street of the town had been reached. There was nobody in sight, but shots were exploding in the lamplight from various concealed points, all of them directed towards the gunsmith's store, from where shots kept spitting back through the shattered front window with steady regularity.

'Conroy's cornered in there,' Mark said. 'He's so busy keeping 'em at bay at the front he can't slip out by the back in case they make a rush forward when he stops firing. Mebbe we'd better take a look round the back for ourselves.'

Big Tony nodded, and both men slipped from their horses.

Guns in hand, they began walking to the side of the

burned-out sheriff's office. Here they tethered their horses and finished their trip to the rear of Halloran's on foot. The back gate was still swinging open, the dead mastiff in the yard. Mark stepped over it and then came to the back door, to find it solidly bolted. He glanced at Big Tony.

'I'm risking it!' Mark snapped, and slammed his gun into the kitchen window, shattering the glass. Then he ducked down and prepared for bullets. None came.

'I get it,' Big Tony said quickly. 'He didn't hear it with all that racket from the firing at the front. Ready to take a chance and go in after him?'

Mark nodded and silently hauled himself up to the sill. Reaching through the smashed glass, he unfastened the catch and slid up the sash, then jumped down into the kitchen. Big Tony quickly joined him and they stood listening to the sound of firing from the store beyond, the door between it and the kitchen being wide open. They both began to glide to the doorway. Then a voice froze them in their tracks.

'*Drop those guns!*'

Mark wheeled and fired at the same time. A shot blazed back at him, and the tearing pain in his shoulder made him realize he'd been hit. Big Tony dropped his gun and stood motionless as a figure loomed out of the shadowy dark. The voice alone proved it was Conroy.

'Buck is holding them at the front,' Conroy explained gloatingly. 'I was figuring on how to escape the back way when you mugs showed up. Now I can get out the front way – with you as my ticket! All right, get moving!'

Mark obeyed, holding his injured shoulder. He found the store beyond was a shambles, the windows gone and the shades in shreds. Halloran and his wife were still bound back to back and gagged, but had managed to roll into a corner. So far they had escaped the flying bullets.

Crouched low behind a big packing case, Buck was firing ceaselessly, possessing an unending supply of ammunition.

'Kill it, Buck,' Conroy ordered. 'We've gotten ourselves a safe-conduct badge.'

Buck glanced around in surprise, then, as he saw Mark and Big Tony both helpless, he grinned and crept away from the packing-case. Outside, there was a lull in the shooting.

'Tell 'em to hold their fire while we get away,' Conroy ordered, jabbing his gun savagely in Mark's ribs.

'Take it easy, fellers,' Mark called through the broken window. 'Mark Dawson here. Conroy's behind me with a gun. If you shoot at him I get it too.'

'Let him come out, Mark. We'll nail him the instant he starts trying to escape and can't get at you.'

'I'm not that crazy,' Conroy shouted back. 'I'm taking the sheriff with me until I'm well clear of the lot of you and if any of you follow I'll. . .'

He got no further. Something shot up from the floor and struck him a violent blow in the face. He was too startled to notice that in the gloom he had trodden on a garden rake that had dropped from Halloran's hardware rack in the midst of the shooting.

Instantly Big Tony flung himself forward and lashed out a terrific uppercut that keeled Conroy straight from his feet and sent him hurtling backwards, bringing down all manner of hardware on top of him.

Buck fired, but the shot went wide. Mark twisted around, bolted into the kitchen, and whipped up Big Tony's gun from where it had fallen on the floor. Dashing straight back into the store he whanged a shot a split second before Buck fired again. Buck took it straight in the chest. He reeled drunkenly, fired without aim, and then stopped another bullet in the stomach. Gulping

156

blood, he twisted around, his gun flying out of his hand. Mark, his face relentless, fired yet again. Buck crashed to the floor, a red hole swelling in his forehead.

Meantime Conroy had struggled up, only to fall promptly back again before another jaw-smashing blow from Big Tony. Before he could get on his feet the towns-folk outside had realized something unexpected had happened and were crowding into the store.

'OK,' Mark said, his voice taut with the pain in his shoulder. 'That heap of manure lying there is Conroy. Wrap him up and dump him with Elias Marlin and the rest of 'em. Take out Buck too, and bury him somewhere. There are more of the hoodlums scattered around town, but we can get them sooner or later, and if they blow the territory, all the better.'

There was a general movement to the boardwalk, with the dazed Conroy in the midst. Mark stood for a time watching the gunsmith and his wife being released, then he looked back at the townsfolk as they triumphantly bore Conroy towards the great barn where the rest of the 'unwanteds' were still imprisoned. Another set of the men kept going, carrying the dead body of Buck, evidently intending to bury it off trail somewhere – without honour and unsung.

'I reckon that's that,' Big Tony said. 'You'd better get back to the Double Triangle, Mark. You want that shoulder fixing.'

Mark began moving, Big Tony helping him along, and at length they regained their horses. Mark found the night air reviving, even though his shoulder was giving him hell.

'You've got Tracey back and you've beaten Conroy and cleared every hoodlum out of town,' Big Tony said. 'What happens next?'

'I collect three hundred thousand dollars!' Mark answered. 'When my uncle died he left me the Double

Triangle, which I'll legally reclaim when I've gotten Marlin's confession that he faked a will. But my uncle also left a private letter in which I was to receive from his Jefferson City lawyers the sum of three hundred thousand dollars *if* – and *only* if – I wiped out the lawlessness ruling Macey's Folly. I gather he'd had his bellyful of it, so left it to me to stamp it out. I was going to split it with Harry and Cliff, only they got themselves killed. So I guess it ought to be split between you, Tracey and me. Only fair. Been mighty tough going at times.'

'I reckon the money's a compensation.' Big Tony grinned as the lights of the Double Triangle appeared in the distance.

'Yeah – and Tracey's a bigger one, if she'll have me. 'Sides, she's lived at the Double Triangle so long it seems only right to me that she should go on doing it.'

Big Tony's grin widened. He knew the answer was not for a moment in doubt.